Table of Contents

Chapter 1: Crossing Paths

The low hum of the restaurant buzzed around Dahlia as she wiped down a corner table, her hands moving automatically through the motions. The usual late-afternoon crowd filled the space, patrons laughing over half-empty glasses, some buried in newspapers, others lingering over desserts they hadn't touched. Through the window, golden light filtered in, casting the room in a warm haze that softened the hard edges of reality. Dahlia stole a quick glance at the clock, watching as the minute hand inched toward the end of her shift.

Just as she turned back to her work, the door chimed, and a gust of cool air swept into the room. She felt it before she saw him—an electric change in the atmosphere, as though the air had thickened. She looked up, and there he was.

Carlos.

He walked with an easy confidence, pausing to survey the room as though he was taking in each detail, his presence undeniable even in the bustling space. It was as if he had a way of bending the room's energy toward him, drawing the light to his silhouette, making everything around him feel blurred, unimportant. He scanned the tables, and then his gaze fell on her. She felt the impact of it immediately, a pull that both thrilled and unsettled her.

Carlos had only been coming to the restaurant for a few weeks, but in that short time, he had slipped into her awareness in a way she hadn't expected. She knew he was young—twenty-five, he'd mentioned casually one afternoon, young enough to make her feel that she should turn away, ignore the way her pulse quickened when he walked in. But there was something magnetic about him. He had that kind of warmth that felt genuine, unaffected, with a hint of charm that seemed both effortless and unintentional.

Without a second thought, she straightened her apron and made her way toward him, weaving through tables with a grace honed from years of working the floor. Her face settled into her usual calm expression, but she could feel her heartbeat picking up, a subtle flutter of nerves she hadn't felt in years.

"Coffee?" she asked, her voice smooth, though she felt the slight tremor in her hands.

Carlos looked up, and a slow smile spread across his face. "Yes, please. Strong, if you can make it."

Dahlia's heart skipped. The way he held her gaze was different from the usual glances she got from customers, who rarely looked beyond the uniform or the apron. There was a curiosity in his eyes, as if he wanted to see past her exterior, into the depths she usually kept hidden. She nodded and turned away, feeling the warmth of his gaze linger on her back.

As she reached the counter, she let out a small breath, chiding herself for the way her thoughts were spiraling. He was just a customer, a man who came for coffee, maybe a quick lunch on his break. Yet each time he walked in, something awakened inside her, a pulse she thought she had lost when she left her old life behind.

Dahlia, you must always protect your heart, her grandmother's voice whispered in her memory, a reminder from another life, another world. In Haiti, love was fierce, not something given freely or without thought. Her grandmother had spoken of it as both a blessing and a curse, a force of nature as unpredictable as the storms that swept across the island, leaving both beauty and destruction in their wake.

It had been over fifteen years since she'd left Haiti, since she had said goodbye to the vibrant world of her childhood and stepped into a new life with Oliver in Alabama. Back then, she had been just twenty, full of hope and dreams for a future that had seemed like a promised land. She'd tried so hard to adapt to her new life, to bury the parts of herself that didn't fit in this new country, where her accent felt thick, her rituals strange, and her memories like ghostly shadows.

Yet here she was, in this small town, married to an American man who had once seemed like the answer to all her questions, her escape from the traditions and expectations of her family. But Oliver had become comfortable, predictable. Their conversations were brief, centered on schedules and bills, not the dreams and passions they once shared. And now, with Carlos sitting just a few feet away, she felt a strange pang of longing, a yearning she couldn't quite explain.

As she poured his coffee, she couldn't shake the memory of her grandmother's words. *Love is not gentle, Dahlia. It is wild, fierce, demanding. It does not yield.* The memory clung to her like the heat of the Haitian sun, and for a brief moment, she felt transported back to her grandmother's small, warm kitchen, filled with the scents of spices and the soft murmurs of old songs.

She returned to Carlos's table, setting the coffee in front of him, their fingers brushing for a fleeting second. The warmth of his touch jolted her, and she felt an electric pull, something primal, something undeniable. Her eyes met his, and in that single glance, she felt a connection that was both exhilarating and terrifying.

"Thank you, Dahlia," he said, and her name sounded different on his lips, like a melody she hadn't heard in years.

The way he lingered on her name made her heart beat faster, a reminder that her name had meaning, that she was more than just a wife, a server, a woman tucked away in a life that felt too small. Here, in this moment, she felt seen, as though Carlos was looking past her carefully crafted facade and seeing the pieces of herself she had long buried.

She turned away, feeling his gaze still on her, but her mind was already racing. She moved through her duties, wiping down tables, greeting customers, but her thoughts kept drifting back to him, to the warmth of his gaze, the quiet intensity in his smile.

As the evening wore on, the restaurant began to empty, and the noise died down to a soft murmur. Dahlia felt the silence settle around her, amplifying every thought, every heartbeat. She stole a glance at Carlos, who was watching her with a calm, steady gaze, as if he had all the time in the world.

When she passed by his table again, he looked up, a faint smile playing on his lips. He gestured to the empty seat across from him, and for a moment, her pulse quickened. It was an innocent invitation, just a seat, but to her, it felt like a crossing of boundaries, a step toward something she wasn't sure she could control.

She hesitated, then sat down, feeling the thrill of the moment, the weight of possibilities unspoken. The hum of the restaurant faded, leaving only the two of them in a quiet world of their own.

"Tell me, Dahlia," he said, his voice low and inviting, "how long have you been here?"

His question was simple, but it cut through her defenses, piercing a part of her she'd kept hidden. "Long enough," she replied, "long enough to know this town doesn't have much to offer."

Carlos chuckled, a sound that sent a shiver down her spine. "Maybe it just needs a little excitement."

Her eyes met his, and for a moment, she felt as if she were standing at the edge of a cliff, looking into a world she had forgotten existed. She wanted to reach out, to feel that thrill, to taste the adventure he seemed to carry with him, to be more than just Dahlia, the server, the wife.

"And what about you, Carlos?" she asked, feeling bold, her voice laced with a hint of mischief. "What brings you to a place like this?"

He shrugged, his gaze never leaving hers. "Maybe I'm here for the same reason. To find something... unexpected."

The words hung between them, charged with a meaning that both of them understood but neither spoke aloud. Dahlia felt her heart race, her thoughts spinning with a mixture of excitement and fear. She could feel the heat of his presence, the subtle magnetism that seemed to pull her toward him, as if the air around them had shifted, thickening with a promise she couldn't ignore.

The last customer left, and the restaurant fell into silence. Outside, the world continued, oblivious to the quiet storm building between them. She felt a pull, an instinctive need to be closer, to let herself be seen, to throw aside the careful walls she had built and step into something raw, something real.

Her grandmother's voice echoed in her mind, a reminder of the power of desire, the danger of forgetting who she was. *Love is fierce, Dahlia. It will claim what it wants, no matter the cost.*

She took a breath, steadying herself. "I should get back to work," she said softly, though the words felt like a lie.

Carlos nodded, but his gaze lingered, as if he knew this was only the beginning, as if he could see the spark she was trying to hide, the yearning she could no longer deny.

As she returned to the counter, her heart still pounding, she felt an awakening within her—a hunger, a desire that whispered promises she had tried to ignore for too long. And though she moved through the motions of her work, she knew that something had shifted irreversibly.

For the first time in years, Dahlia felt truly alive, bound by an invisible thread to a stranger who felt more like a missing piece than a passing shadow. The walls of her carefully built life began to blur, leaving only the faint echo.

Chapter 2: A Life of Compromise

The day began as every other one did, with Dahlia navigating her small, predictable routine in the quiet solitude of dawn. In the silence of her kitchen, the sound of the coffee maker filled the air as she waited, leaning against the counter, her eyes half-closed. She tried to savor the rich scent of coffee as it brewed, the one small indulgence that still stirred something within her. The aroma brought back mornings from her childhood, memories of her grandmother grinding beans by hand, adding the faintest touch of cinnamon, filling their home with a warmth and a comfort that felt as essential as breathing.

As the coffee filled her cup, she sighed, staring into the dark liquid, almost hoping it would reveal something, like an oracle of some kind. She had begun to wonder how her life had narrowed into this routine, the predictable path she once found so reassuring now felt like a slow erasure of herself. Oliver, her husband, had already left for work, leaving a silence behind that had become all too familiar. He'd sent her the same brief message he sent every morning: *Have a good day.* The words stared up at her from her phone, impersonal and yet obligatory, a habit born of years together but absent of feeling.

She typed back, *You too,* and set her phone down, knowing there'd be no reply. Sometimes, she missed the man he used to be—the Oliver who had made her laugh, who would leave silly notes for her to find, whose warmth once felt like home. But now their life had settled into quiet, separate orbits, two people bound by habit rather than connection. It was as if the light in their relationship had dimmed gradually, so slowly that she hadn't noticed it until it was almost gone.

Sipping her coffee, Dahlia stared out the window, her gaze lost in the quiet, empty street. But her thoughts drifted somewhere else, somewhere vivid and electric: Carlos. She hadn't seen him in days, but his image lingered in her mind, clear and sharp. The warmth of his smile, the depth of his gaze that seemed to notice everything about her. It was a dangerous habit, letting her thoughts linger on him like this, and she chastised herself, yet she couldn't quite stop. He was a spark in her otherwise dimmed world, a reminder of a part of herself she had buried, the part that still wanted more.

She dressed in a soft, sage-green blouse, one that Oliver had once complimented years ago but hadn't noticed in ages. She caught her reflection in the mirror and adjusted the neckline, smoothing her hair. It felt strange, dressing with a sense of anticipation, a quiet thrill she hadn't felt in years, but she let herself indulge in it, just for a moment. In the back of her mind, she could hear her grandmother's voice, her soft words warning her to tread carefully, to guard her heart against desires that might consume her.

But as she walked the familiar route to the restaurant, Dahlia pushed those thoughts away, focusing instead on the hum of the street, the soft morning breeze that stirred the leaves on the trees, the distant chatter of early commuters. She liked these quiet moments, the way the world felt half-awake, wrapped in the softness of morning light. Yet today, everything felt sharper, more alive. She could feel her heart beating a little faster with each step, anticipation growing in her chest.

When she reached the restaurant, the usual morning crowd was already there, regulars in their usual places. She greeted them with a smile, the easy warmth she wore like a mask, but her mind was elsewhere, caught in the quiet hope that Carlos would walk through the door. As she prepared coffee at the counter, she glanced at the door more times than she cared to admit, each time chiding herself for the flutter of excitement that rose within her.

Then, as if summoned by her thoughts, he walked in. The sight of him caught her off guard, and for a moment, she felt breathless, her pulse quickening. Carlos moved through the doorway, shrugging off his jacket, his gaze sweeping across the room before landing on her. The corners of his mouth lifted in that faint, knowing smile, and she felt her cheeks warm, a thrill that she couldn't hide.

He walked over, and she noted the way he moved, casual yet assured, as if the world shifted to accommodate his presence. He leaned against the counter, looking at her with a quiet intensity that made her feel seen in a way she hadn't felt in years.

"Good morning, Dahlia," he said, his voice low and smooth, the words rolling off his tongue like an invitation.

"Good morning, Carlos," she replied, hoping her voice sounded steady. Her hands moved instinctively as she reached for a cup, though her mind felt anything but steady. "Coffee, right?"

He nodded, but he didn't look away. His gaze lingered on her, as if he were trying to read her, to see past the surface. "You look... different this morning. Lighter, maybe?"

The comment caught her off guard, and she felt a blush creep up her neck, a thrill in the idea that he'd noticed the small changes, that he saw her as more than just a face behind the counter. She poured his coffee, focusing on the steady stream, anything to avoid his eyes. "I don't think I've changed much," she said softly, but her heart told her otherwise.

He tilted his head, a smile playing at the edges of his mouth. "I'd argue otherwise."

His words hung in the air between them, laced with a warmth and curiosity that felt intoxicating. She placed the coffee in front of him, her fingers brushing his as she did. The touch was fleeting, yet it sent a shiver through her, as though a hidden current had passed between them.

"So, tell me," he said, his voice softer now, leaning in as if to share a secret, "where did you grow up, Dahlia?"

The question took her by surprise. People rarely asked about her life outside of her role here, rarely probed into her past. Her throat tightened, but there was a part of her that longed to answer, to let him in. "Haiti," she replied, her voice barely more than a whisper.

His gaze held hers, a softness in his eyes that felt almost like understanding. "I imagine it's beautiful there."

A wistful smile tugged at her lips. "It is... everything is alive, vibrant. The colors, the sounds... it's hard to explain." For a moment, she was back there, in the narrow streets of her village, the sun beating down on her as she ran through fields, her laughter mingling with the sounds of the marketplace.

"Do you ever miss it?" Carlos asked, his tone gentle, as if sensing the weight of her memories.

She nodded, feeling a pang of longing she hadn't allowed herself to feel in years. "Sometimes," she admitted, "but that was... another life."

He watched her, his gaze steady, and for the first time, she felt seen, truly seen. In his eyes, she glimpsed the woman she once was, the woman she had been before she became a wife, a worker, a figure bound by the quiet compromises of everyday life. She wanted to say more, to tell him about the life she'd left behind, about the things she'd lost, but the words felt heavy, caught in her throat.

As the morning wore on, their conversations flowed, easy and light, yet filled with an undercurrent of something deeper. He stayed longer than usual, sipping his coffee slowly, his gaze lingering on her with a warmth that made her heart race. She found herself drawn to him, each word, each smile pulling her deeper into a world where she felt alive, where her heart beat with a vibrancy she had almost forgotten.

When he finally stood to leave, he looked at her, a gentle smile on his lips. "Thank you for the coffee, Dahlia. I'll see you tomorrow?"

The words filled her with a quiet thrill, a promise that felt as dangerous as it was enticing. She nodded, unable to find her voice, and watched as he walked out, leaving her with a sense of longing that settled deep within her, a hunger that wouldn't be easily quelled.

For the rest of the day, she moved through her routine, her mind drifting back to him, to the way he had looked at her, to the feeling of his hand brushing hers. She knew it was foolish, a spark that could easily turn into a wildfire, but the thought of him lingered, impossible to shake. In his presence, she had felt something awaken, a part of herself she had thought was lost forever, hidden beneath years of compromise and routine.

And as the day wore on, she realized she didn't want to let that feeling go. She wanted more—more than the quiet, comfortable life she had settled into, more than the role she had grown to accept.

Her grandmother's voice echoed in her mind, a warning wrapped in love. *Love is fierce, Dahlia. It will claim what it wants, no matter the cost.*

Dahlia took a deep breath, feeling the weight of her choices pressing against her, yet a small, dangerous smile tugged at her lips. She was standing on the edge of something new, something thrilling and unknown. And though she knew the risks, the line she was inching closer to crossing, she abandoned the thought, pulled instead toward the thrill that Carlos seemed to bring into her life. Every glance, every smile, each unspoken word had begun to chip away at the life she had carefully built. She didn't know what she was doing, didn't understand why she felt this pull to a man who, in another world, would have been just a stranger she'd pass by without a second glance.

The evening sun dipped low as her shift came to a close, and she began to close up, the clinking of dishes and the soft shuffle of chairs filling the space as she worked. The day had passed in a blur, every moment marked by thoughts of him, the lingering scent of his cologne, the warmth of his gaze, the subtle curve of his smile. She felt herself drifting back to their brief conversation, replaying each word, each glance as though they held some hidden meaning.

She was nearly finished when the door chimed softly, the last rays of light catching in the glass, casting a warm glow across the room. For a moment, she thought she was alone, lost in her thoughts. But then she turned, and there he was, standing in the doorway, silhouetted by the fading sunlight.

Carlos had returned.

The sight of him standing there, waiting, sent a thrill racing through her. She felt her breath catch, her heart stuttering in her chest as he walked toward her, a slow, measured stride that spoke of quiet confidence. The room felt smaller, the air charged with an unspoken tension that seemed to thicken as he came closer, his eyes fixed on hers with an intensity that made her feel exposed, vulnerable.

"Didn't expect to see you again tonight," she said, her voice barely above a whisper.

He smiled, a soft, almost mischievous grin that made her pulse race. "Thought I'd stop by, see if you needed any help closing up."

She laughed, though the sound felt foreign, her own voice strange in her ears. "I think I've got it covered. But... thanks for the offer."

He nodded, a spark in his eyes that made her feel as if there was more he wanted to say, something lingering just beneath the surface, unspoken but palpable. They stood there, caught in the quiet space between words, the sounds of the world fading away as they looked at each other, a moment that stretched out, heavy with possibilities.

Finally, he broke the silence, his voice low, almost a murmur. "You know, Dahlia, there's something different about you. Something I haven't seen in anyone else."

The words hung between them, and she felt a shiver run down her spine, a thrill that made her pulse quicken. She didn't know what he saw in her, didn't understand why he seemed drawn to her in the same way she was to him. But in that moment, she felt alive, more alive than she had in years, as though she was standing on the edge of something profound, something that could change everything.

"Maybe I've just... forgotten who I am," she replied, the words spilling out before she could stop them, a confession she hadn't meant to make.

He stepped closer, his gaze steady, unwavering. "Then maybe it's time you remembered."

The air between them felt electric, charged with an intensity that made her feel as though she were on the verge of something dangerous, something that could pull her under if she let it. And in that moment, she realized that she wanted to let it, wanted to feel the thrill of something new, something that made her heart race and her soul ache with a longing she could barely understand.

Without another word, he reached out, his hand grazing hers, a touch so light it felt like a whisper, yet it sent a shiver through her, a spark that ignited something deep within. She looked up at him, her breath caught in her throat, and for the first time, she felt as though she were truly seen, truly known, in a way that went beyond words, beyond reason.

And in that moment, she knew that there was no going back, that whatever path she had been on had shifted, drawn into the orbit of something she couldn't control, something that would change her forever.

The world outside was fading, the last rays of sunlight slipping below the horizon, casting the room in a soft, golden glow. And as they stood there, caught in the quiet intensity of that moment, she felt her heart racing, a thrill coursing through her veins, a hunger she hadn't felt in years.

This was only the beginning, she realized, the first step on a path that would lead her somewhere new, somewhere unknown. And though she didn't know what lay ahead, she knew that she was ready, ready to embrace whatever this was, to follow the spark that had been ignited within her, wherever it might lead.

Chapter 3: The Line Between Right and Wrong

The morning light was just beginning to seep into the sky, casting a muted, soft glow over Dahlia's small home as she lay awake in bed, listening to the rhythm of Oliver's breathing beside her. She watched the way the light filtered through the blinds, a delicate pattern tracing lines across the ceiling, as though marking the boundaries she knew she shouldn't cross. But her thoughts had already drifted elsewhere, drawn to the memory of Carlos's voice, the way he had looked at her with a softness that held something deeper—a hint of mystery, of promise.

She lay still, her mind replaying fragments of their conversations, each word like a subtle stroke on her heart. He had seemed to understand something about her that even she had forgotten—a part of herself that had been dulled by routine, hidden beneath the weight of years and silence. She wondered if he had noticed the longing in her gaze, the way she lingered on his every word, as if he held a key to something she couldn't name.

The scent of coffee drifted from the kitchen, faint and comforting, and she knew Oliver was already up, moving through the same quiet motions he did every morning. She closed her eyes for a moment, savoring the last remnants of her thoughts before they dissolved into the steady pulse of her daily life.

Get up, Dahlia, she told herself, forcing her feet to touch the cool floor. *Don't let your mind wander.*

As she dressed, her fingers brushed against the soft fabric of her blouse, a deep green she hadn't worn in years. She glanced at herself in the mirror, startled by the intensity in her own eyes, the flush in her cheeks that hadn't been there just days ago. There was a small thrill in choosing that blouse, a quiet rebellion against the safe, muted colors she usually wore.

She moved to the kitchen, where Oliver sat at the small table, his gaze fixed on the newspaper. His fingers turned the pages methodically, each flick of his wrist a reminder of the life they had settled into—a life of routines, of quiet companionship, but absent of the spark that once drew them together. She watched him for a moment, studying his profile, the slight furrow in his brow as he read, and she felt a pang of something she couldn't name, a mixture of affection and a deep, aching sadness.

"Good morning," she said, forcing a smile.

Oliver looked up, his eyes meeting hers for just a second before drifting back to the paper. "Morning," he replied, his tone warm but distant, as if the words were spoken out of habit rather than connection.

They sat together in silence, the weight of unspoken words pressing down on her as she sipped her coffee. She could feel the walls of their life closing in around her, the edges of their world growing smaller with each passing day. And yet, even in the quiet comfort of his presence, her thoughts slipped back to Carlos, to the way he had looked at her with that soft, knowing smile.

She wondered what it would be like to sit across from him like this, in the quiet of the morning, his gaze steady and warm, his voice filling the empty spaces in her heart. The thought sent a thrill through her, a ripple of excitement that left her feeling breathless, and she quickly pushed it away, reminding herself of the life she had chosen, the promises she had made.

But as she walked to work, her mind kept returning to him, each step bringing her closer to the restaurant and the possibility of seeing him again. She tried to shake the feeling, to tell herself it was just a fleeting attraction, something that would pass if she ignored it. But deep down, she knew it was more than that—Carlos had awakened something within her, a spark that had been buried beneath years of compromise, of settling for a life that felt safe but empty.

The restaurant was quiet when she arrived, the early morning light casting long shadows across the empty tables. She moved through the motions of setting up, her hands moving automatically, yet her mind was somewhere else, lost in the memory of his gaze, the warmth of his hand brushing hers. She felt as if she were standing on the edge of something vast and unknown, a world that beckoned to her with promises of freedom, of passion, of a life that felt alive.

The door chimed, breaking her reverie, and she looked up to see Carlos standing there, his gaze already fixed on her. He walked toward her with that same easy confidence, his smile warm and familiar, yet tinged with something deeper, something that made her heart race.

"Morning, Dahlia," he said, his voice soft, as if the words were meant just for her.

"Good morning, Carlos," she replied, her voice barely a whisper, her pulse quickening at the sound of his name on her lips.

He leaned against the counter, close enough that she could feel the warmth of his presence, the faint scent of his cologne mingling with the aroma of coffee. "Busy morning?" he asked, his tone casual, yet his gaze held an intensity that made her feel as though he could see right through her, past the walls she had built around herself.

"Not yet," she replied, forcing a smile, though her hands trembled slightly as she reached for a coffee cup. "But it's early."

He watched her, his gaze lingering on her with a warmth that felt almost tangible, like a touch. "It suits you," he said quietly. "Being here. You seem... at ease."

The comment took her by surprise, and she felt a blush rise to her cheeks, a mixture of pleasure and embarrassment. "It's just work," she replied, her voice unsteady. "Nothing special."

He tilted his head, studying her with a softness that made her heart ache. "Sometimes, the simplest things reveal the most about us."

The words settled over her like a gentle weight, and she felt herself drawn to him, a pull that went beyond attraction, something that felt like fate, like destiny. She wanted to tell him everything—to share the dreams she had buried, the life she had left behind, the woman she had once been. But the words stayed locked within her, a secret she couldn't bear to share, not yet.

They fell into a comfortable silence, and she found herself drawn to the warmth of his presence, the quiet intensity that seemed to wrap around her like a promise. For the first time in years, she felt alive, her heart beating with a rhythm that matched the quiet thrill of his gaze, the unspoken bond that had formed between them, fragile yet undeniable.

When he finally left, the world felt a little dimmer, the restaurant colder in his absence. She moved through her shift in a haze, her mind drifting back to him, to the warmth of his gaze, the spark that had ignited within her, a spark she knew she couldn't ignore. And as she closed up that night, the memory of him lingered, filling the empty spaces of her life with a warmth she hadn't felt in years.

Walking home, she felt a strange sense of peace, a quiet joy that settled over her like a blanket. The streets were quiet, the world wrapped in the soft glow of twilight, and for a moment, she felt as though she were standing on the edge of something vast and unknown, a world that beckoned to her with promises of freedom, of passion, of a life that felt alive.

When she reached her house, she paused on the porch, her gaze drifting over the familiar landscape of her life. She could see Oliver inside, his figure framed by the soft glow of the kitchen light, and she felt a pang of guilt, a reminder of the life she had chosen, the man she had promised to love.

But as she stood there, her thoughts drifted back to Carlos, to the warmth of his gaze, the quiet intensity that had wrapped around her like a promise. And she knew that something had shifted within her, a spark that had been ignited, a hunger that wouldn't be easily quenched.

Inside, she moved through the familiar motions, her hands steady as she prepared dinner, her heart racing with the memory of him, the way he had looked at her, as though she were someone worth seeing, worth knowing.

And as she lay in bed that night, listening to the steady rhythm of Oliver's breathing, she felt the quiet thrill of possibility settle over her, a promise of something new, something thrilling, something that made her feel alive.

She closed her eyes, letting herself be drawn into the memory of Carlos, the warmth of his gaze, the quiet intensity that seemed to wrap around her like a promise. And as she drifted into sleep, she knew that she was already lost, drawn into the orbit of something she couldn't escape, something that would change her forever.

Chapter 4: The First Step Over the Line

The night felt charged, as though the universe itself had conspired to wrap the world in a veil of mystery, drawing her forward. Dahlia's footsteps echoed softly along the empty sidewalks as she made her way to the bar she knew Carlos frequented. Every step seemed a little louder, a little heavier, like a heartbeat marking each moment, each decision she was about to make.

She had never done anything like this before—never followed an impulse so wild, so dangerous, and yet she felt irresistibly drawn to him, a pull that defied logic. She told herself it was innocent, a simple curiosity, but deep down, she knew it was more than that. She wasn't seeking a drink or a casual conversation; she was seeking something real, something that would make her feel alive.

As she approached the bar, she hesitated, her heart pounding. The warm light spilling from the windows cast inviting glows on the cobblestones beneath her feet, but she could feel the weight of her decision, the line she was about to cross. She thought of Oliver, his steady presence, the life they had built together. The guilt prickled at her, tugging at the edges of her mind, but she pushed it away, her gaze fixed on the warm light inside. For once, she wanted to forget the woman she was supposed to be and embrace the woman she felt awakening within her.

Taking a deep breath, she pushed open the door and stepped inside.

Dahlia could feel her heart hammering as she entered the bar, the warmth and dim lighting cloaking her in a sense of intimacy and daring she hadn't felt in years. Her gaze swept the room until it landed on Carlos. He was leaning casually at the far end of the bar, his eyes flickering with amusement as he spoke with the bartender. Just the sight of him felt like a spark to her system, setting her pulse racing.

As though sensing her presence, Carlos looked up, his gaze meeting hers across the room. A smile spread slowly across his face, warm and inviting, his eyes holding an unspoken question. She hesitated, then moved toward him, each step an act of defiance against the careful life she had constructed.

"Dahlia," he said softly as she reached him, his voice wrapping around her like a familiar warmth. "What a surprise."

"Surprise?" she replied, tilting her head with a sly smile. "I could say the same about you."

He chuckled, motioning for her to join him. "Well, now I feel lucky. Two surprises in one night."

They ordered drinks, and as they waited, the silence between them grew thick with unspoken words, an almost tangible tension. Finally, Carlos broke it, leaning in a little closer, his gaze searching hers.

"So, what brings you out here tonight?" he asked, his voice low, as if they were sharing a secret.

Dahlia hesitated, her mind racing as she considered her answer. She knew she could give him a safe, casual reply, something that would keep her firmly within the lines she had drawn for herself. But instead, she felt a flicker of boldness, a need to let the night unfold without caution.

"Maybe I needed a break from being good," she said, her voice softer, more intimate. Her eyes met his, and she felt a thrill as she saw the spark of intrigue flicker in his gaze.

"Good?" Carlos murmured, his smile widening. "I never pictured you as just... 'good.'"

She laughed softly, feeling herself slipping into an ease she hadn't felt in ages. "No? Then what did you picture me as?"

He tilted his head, studying her with a newfound intensity, his eyes tracing her face as if seeing her for the first time. "I don't know yet," he admitted, his voice barely above a whisper. "But I feel like there's more to you than you let on. Like you've been hiding."

Her breath caught at his words. She hadn't expected him to see through her so clearly, to sense the parts of herself she had kept buried. A memory stirred within her, of her grandmother's old saying about the power and fire of a woman's heart. She had thought she left that side of herself in Haiti, wrapped up in the quiet mystery of her past. But here, under Carlos's gaze, she felt it waking, slipping out from the shadows.

"You're not wrong," she replied, her voice laced with a hint of mystery. She leaned in, close enough to feel the warmth radiating from him, her eyes holding his. "But sometimes it's safer to keep certain parts hidden."

Carlos smiled, a faint hint of challenge in his eyes. "Is that a warning or an invitation?"

"Maybe both," she whispered, her lips curving into a playful smile. She let her fingers trail along the edge of her glass, watching as his gaze followed the movement, an unspoken hunger flickering in his eyes. She could feel the shift between them, the intensity deepening, like a current pulling them both in.

He took a sip of his drink, his eyes never leaving hers. "You know, Dahlia," he murmured, his voice laced with intrigue, "I had a feeling you weren't as simple as you seemed."

She laughed softly, the sound low and throaty, surprising herself with the sensuality in her own voice. "Simple?" she echoed, leaning closer until their faces were only inches apart. "I don't think I've ever been accused of that before."

Carlos's smile widened, and she could see the interest in his gaze deepen, a look that sent a thrill through her, awakening something wild and unapologetic within her. "Good," he replied, his voice like velvet. "Because I don't think I could be interested in simple."

The words lingered between them, a subtle invitation, and she felt herself drawn into his orbit, the warmth of his presence wrapping around her like a cloak. She reached out, her hand lightly touching his arm, her fingers lingering longer than necessary. She could feel his heartbeat through his sleeve, a steady, reassuring rhythm that seemed to pull her in, grounding her while igniting every nerve in her body.

"Tell me, Carlos," she murmured, her voice low, almost a whisper. "What do you think I'm hiding?"

He tilted his head, considering her, his gaze sliding over her with an intensity that left her breathless. "I think... you're hiding a fire," he replied, his voice soft but charged with an unspoken challenge. "Something that's been locked away for too long."

A smile played on her lips, and she felt a surge of confidence, a boldness she hadn't known in years. "Maybe it's because no one's dared to unlock it."

Carlos's eyes darkened, his smile shifting into something deeper, something that held a hint of promise. "Then maybe it's time," he murmured, his voice barely audible, "for someone to take that risk."

Their gazes locked, and for a moment, it was as if the rest of the world faded away, leaving only the two of them, wrapped in the intensity of the moment. She could feel her heart pounding, her pulse racing, and she knew that they were teetering on the edge of something that went beyond words, beyond reason. A tension hummed between them, a quiet, powerful energy that seemed to draw them closer with each passing second.

Without thinking, she leaned in, her hand brushing against his, her fingers tracing a gentle path along his wrist. "Maybe you should," she whispered, her voice a soft, daring challenge.

Carlos's gaze flickered, his eyes smoldering as he reached up, his fingers brushing a strand of hair behind her ear, his touch lingering against her skin. The warmth of his hand sent a shiver down her spine, a thrill that left her breathless, caught between fear and desire.

In a bold move, she let her hand slide up his arm, resting just above his elbow. She could feel the muscles beneath her fingers, the strength in his grip, and it sent a thrill through her, a sense of danger and excitement she hadn't felt in years.

"I don't know what it is about you, Dahlia," he murmured, his voice like a caress. "But I can't seem to stay away."

She laughed softly, her lips curving into a playful smile. "Maybe it's the same thing that's drawing me to you," she replied, her voice barely above a whisper. "The thrill of the unknown... and the risk."

Carlos's hand moved to her face, his fingers tracing the line of her jaw, his touch soft and intimate. "Then maybe we should stop pretending this is innocent," he murmured, his eyes holding hers with a heat that left her breathless.

She felt herself leaning into him, her lips just a whisper away from his, her heart pounding as she gave in to the pull between them. And then, in a moment of daring, she closed the distance, her lips brushing against his in a kiss that was soft, tentative, but quickly deepened, igniting a passion that she hadn't known in years.

Their kiss was electric, a release of everything they had been holding back, a connection that went beyond words, beyond reason. She could feel his hands moving to her waist, pulling her closer, his touch firm and reassuring, a steady anchor in the whirlwind of emotions that had been unleashed.

When they finally pulled apart, her breath was shallow, her heart racing as she looked up at him, her gaze meeting his with a mixture of excitement and fear. She knew, in that moment, that they had crossed a line, that there was no going back. And as she stood there, caught in his gaze, she felt a thrill of anticipation, a hunger that she hadn't felt in years, a promise of something more.

Carlos smiled, his hand lingering on her waist, his gaze soft and warm. "Whatever this is, Dahlia," he murmured, his voice a quiet, steady promise, "I don't think it's something either of us can ignore."

She smiled, her heart fluttering at his words, feeling the weight of his gaze, the intensity of his presence wrapping around her like a warm, protective cloak. And in that moment, she knew that she was ready to embrace whatever came next, to step into the unknown with him, to let herself be drawn into a world of passion and mystery, a world where she could finally be free.

The night around them was quiet, filled with possibilities, and as they left the bar together, Dahlia felt a thrill that went beyond words, a sense of liberation that left her breathless. This was only the beginning, she realized, the first step into a world where she could finally feel alive, finally embrace the woman she had kept hidden for so long.

And as they walked together into the night, Dahlia felt a lightness in her step, an intoxicating feeling that bubbled up as she walked alongside Carlos, her arm brushing his, their shoulders touching in a quiet, comforting rhythm. She let herself savor the closeness, the warmth of his presence beside her, the way the night air felt charged, alive with a promise she hadn't realized she was waiting for.

"Tell me something," Carlos murmured, breaking the silence as they walked. "What would you do if you could have one night—no rules, no regrets?"

The question hung in the air, weighty and bold, daring her to imagine a life beyond her safe, predictable world. She looked over at him, her lips curving into a soft, daring smile. "One night?" she echoed, the thrill of the idea shimmering in her voice. "I suppose... I'd be fearless. I'd forget every rule I've ever been told and listen only to my own heart."

Carlos's gaze softened, a flicker of something deeper, something raw, passing over his face. "Then maybe tonight should be that night," he whispered, his voice barely a breath between them.

The words stirred something within her, a fierce, wild energy she had long buried beneath layers of duty and expectation. She laughed, a low, throaty sound that felt foreign yet freeing, and met his gaze, her eyes reflecting the same hunger, the same desire. "Then let's see where this night takes us."

They wandered through the city streets, the lights casting golden pools on the ground, their laughter mingling with the soft sounds of the city around them. The world felt smaller, more intimate, as though they were the only two people who mattered, bound by the secret they shared and the unspoken words that filled the spaces between them.

When they reached the river, Carlos stopped, turning to face her, his hands slipping gently around her waist. His touch was gentle, grounding, yet she could feel the electricity humming just beneath the surface, a pulse that matched her own. The quiet sound of the water lapping against the banks blended with the rustling leaves overhead, creating a cocoon of intimacy that wrapped around them, holding them close.

"Dahlia," he murmured, his voice a gentle caress, his eyes dark and intense. "Tell me what you want."

Her heart raced at his words, a thrill coursing through her as she felt her own desires surfacing, free from restraint, free from doubt. "I want..." She took a breath, steadying herself, her voice low and unsteady. "I want you, Carlos," she murmured, her voice barely more than a breath. "I want all of you."

He didn't respond with words; he couldn't. Instead, he let his actions speak for him, his hands tracing the curves of her body, memorizing every inch, every line, every detail as though he were discovering her for the first time, as though this were the only moment that mattered. They moved together in a rhythm that was both slow and urgent, a rhythm that spoke of the restraint they had both held onto for so long, a restraint that had finally broken, leaving them both free to explore the depths of their connection.

They stood there by the river, wrapped in each other, the night closing around them like a secret, a promise that lingered in the quiet darkness. In his arms, Dahlia felt her world shift, the lines of her life redrawn, leaving only the raw, undeniable truth of her own desires, her own heart.

And in that moment, with the city lights flickering behind them and the river flowing steadily past, she knew that this was the beginning of something she could no longer resist—an awakening, a love, a life that would change her forever.

Chapter 5: The Return to Reality

Dahlia slipped quietly into her house, the early morning sun casting a golden glow across the walls, illuminating familiar shadows in an unfamiliar way. The soft warmth of dawn felt different, almost intrusive, breaking through the spell of the night she had just left behind. Her fingers brushed against the cool surface of the door, and she lingered there, letting the memory of Carlos linger on her skin, in her breath, in the faint pulse that still thrummed within her.

The house was silent, thick with a stillness that felt like judgment. She could feel it in the walls, in the carefully placed furniture, in the soft hum of the refrigerator in the kitchen—everything in her home seemed to echo a question she wasn't ready to answer. Her gaze drifted over the quiet room, the shadows stretching long across the floor, as if trying to reach her, to hold her in place.

Her heart raced as she stepped further inside, each step deliberate, careful, as though she were afraid to disturb the space she had claimed as hers. She could feel the weight of her decisions pressing down on her, the echoes of her own heartbeat seeming to fill the room, but there was a quiet exhilaration thrumming beneath it all, a pulse that had been awakened and was now alive within her, unstoppable.

What have I done?

The question flickered in her mind, soft and persistent, but she ignored it, brushing it aside as she made her way to the kitchen, her footsteps soft against the floor. Oliver was still asleep, and the thought brought a strange mix of relief and guilt, an emotion she couldn't quite name.

Her hand rested on the countertop as she steadied herself, her fingers tracing the cool, smooth surface, grounding herself. But as she closed her eyes, the memories flooded back, unbidden—the warmth of Carlos's hands on her skin, the intensity in his gaze, the way his voice had wrapped around her, filling her with a sense of being seen, of being truly alive.

She poured herself a glass of water, the cold liquid sliding down her throat, shocking her senses back to the present. But the taste of him lingered, a faint, intoxicating memory that she couldn't shake, that she didn't want to shake. She pressed her fingers to her lips, feeling the ghost of his kiss, a warmth that spread through her, a quiet fire that seemed to burn beneath the surface, hidden yet undeniable.

The guilt stirred again, a quiet whisper that grew louder with each passing second, but even as it gnawed at her, she couldn't deny the thrill that had settled within her, a warmth that refused to fade. She felt as though she were standing on the edge of a cliff, the ground beneath her crumbling, yet she couldn't bring herself to step back.

She was drawn to the edge, to the unknown, to the promise of something more, something real.

As she took a deep breath, her phone buzzed softly in her pocket, the sudden vibration jolting her back to the present. She pulled it out, her heart skipping as she saw Carlos's name on the screen, a message that was simple yet filled with unspoken promise: *"Thinking of last night. Can we meet again?"*

The words sent a thrill through her, a quiet excitement that pulsed in her veins, mingling with the guilt and the fear, creating a cocktail of emotions that left her breathless, torn. She glanced toward the bedroom, where Oliver lay sleeping, oblivious to the storm brewing within her, to the secrets she held close.

Dahlia's fingers hovered over the screen, her mind racing with the possibilities, the risks, the thrill of what could be. She typed a reply, her pulse quickening with each word, her fingers trembling with anticipation. *"Yes. Tonight."*

She hit send, her heart racing as the message disappeared, a promise that hung in the air, filling the room with a sense of anticipation, a quiet electricity that seemed to charge every breath. She closed her eyes, letting herself feel the thrill, the warmth, the hunger that had been awakened, a need that she couldn't deny, that she didn't want to deny.

The day passed in a haze, each moment blurring into the next as she went through the motions of her life, her thoughts consumed by the night to come, by the promise of Carlos's touch, his gaze, his voice that had wrapped around her like a secret, a confession. She felt as though she were moving through a dream, each step a quiet defiance against the life she had built, a life that felt too small, too safe, too quiet.

Oliver's presence was a steady weight, a reminder of the choices she had made, the promises she had kept. He moved through the day with his usual ease, his gentle smile, his steady hands, his quiet warmth that had once felt like home but now seemed distant, like a memory that had faded over time.

"Are you alright?" he asked softly, his gaze searching hers as they sat together at the breakfast table, the morning light casting a soft glow across his face.

The question caught her off guard, and she forced a smile, nodding as she looked away, unable to meet his gaze. "Just tired," she replied, her voice soft, careful, as though she were trying to hold something back, to keep her secrets hidden.

He nodded, accepting her answer with the same quiet understanding he had always shown, and a pang of guilt tightened her chest, a reminder of the life they had built together, a life she had chosen. But even as the guilt stirred within her, she felt the pull of Carlos, a quiet, insistent hum that lingered beneath the surface, a hunger that refused to be ignored.

The hours slipped by, each one a reminder of the choices she had made, of the path she was walking, a path that felt both thrilling and dangerous, a line she couldn't uncross. And as the day turned to evening, she found herself standing in front of the mirror, studying her reflection, searching for the woman she had become, the woman who had dared to defy the life she had known.

Her fingers brushed against her collarbone, tracing the line of her neck, a memory of Carlos's touch, the warmth of his hand, the heat of his gaze that had seemed to see through her, to the very core of her. She felt a surge of confidence, a boldness that left her breathless, a readiness to step fully into this new life, this new self that had been waiting, hidden, for so long.

As she slipped out the door, her heart raced, her thoughts a jumble of anticipation and fear, a thrill that left her breathless, alive. She knew the risks, understood the consequences, but in that moment, none of it mattered. She was alive, truly alive, and for the first time in years, she was ready to embrace whatever came next.

The night air was cool, a soft breeze brushing against her skin as she made her way to the place they had agreed to meet, her heart pounding with each step, her pulse a steady rhythm that echoed the anticipation thrumming within her. The world felt sharper, more vibrant, as though every sound, every shadow held a secret, a promise, a thrill that she couldn't resist.

Carlos was waiting for her, his figure silhouetted against the streetlight, a faint smile playing on his lips as he watched her approach. She felt the heat of his gaze, a warmth that wrapped around her, pulling her in, grounding her, even as it left her breathless, on edge.

"Dahlia," he murmured, his voice soft, intimate, as though her name were a secret meant only for him.

"Carlos," she replied, her voice a whisper, her gaze meeting his, a spark flickering between them, a connection that felt undeniable, unbreakable.

They stood there for a moment, the silence stretching between them, heavy with unspoken words, with promises, with a hunger that had been awakened, a fire that refused to be extinguished. And as he reached for her, his hand warm against her skin, she felt herself surrendering, letting go of the life she had known, stepping fully into the world they had created, a world that was wild, dangerous, thrilling.

Their night together unfolded in a dance of passion and restraint, a rhythm that left her breathless, alive, her senses heightened, her soul awakened. She felt as though she were seeing the world for the first time, each touch, each kiss, each whispered word a promise, a confession, a truth that she had been waiting to claim.

And as the dawn broke, casting a golden glow over the city, she knew that there was no going back, no returning to the life she had known. She was changed, transformed, a woman who had tasted freedom, passion, a love that was wild and unrestrained.

She slipped out quietly, her heart racing, her thoughts a tangled web of emotion, of guilt, of hunger. She knew the risks, understood the consequences, but in that moment, none of it mattered. She was alive, truly alive, and for the first time in years, she felt as though she were finally living, finally free.

Chapter 6: The Point of No Return

The tension in the house was thick as Dahlia closed the door behind her, her hand lingering on the handle, every instinct telling her to turn and leave. She could feel the weight of Oliver's gaze from across the room, the unspoken questions filling the silence between them. He was seated at the kitchen table, his hands clasped tightly, his face half-shadowed in the dim light, but she could see the resolve in his eyes, the simmering anger barely contained.

"Dahlia," he said, his voice low, firm. "Sit down. We need to talk."

She swallowed, a sense of dread creeping over her as she crossed the room, feeling his gaze on her with every step. She sat opposite him, her hands resting on the edge of the table, tense, her pulse racing as she braced herself for what was coming.

He took a deep breath, his gaze piercing, unwavering. "Where have you been?"

The question was simple, direct, but it held a weight that left her breathless. She opened her mouth, a thousand excuses flitting through her mind, but she knew they would sound hollow, empty in the face of his scrutiny.

"Out," she replied, her voice barely more than a whisper. She avoided his gaze, her fingers twisting nervously in her lap.

"Out?" he repeated, his tone laced with disbelief, hurt. "Dahlia, don't insult me. You've been gone for nights, coming home at odd hours, avoiding me, lying to my face." His voice cracked, a raw vulnerability seeping into his words. "I deserve the truth."

She felt the guilt twist in her chest, sharp and unrelenting, but even as she met his gaze, the memories of her nights with Carlos lingered, a quiet thrill that pulsed beneath the surface. She could feel herself slipping, torn between the life she had built and the life she had tasted in those stolen hours.

"Oliver," she murmured, her voice soft, pleading. "I didn't mean to hurt you. I just... I needed something. Something I couldn't find here."

His face contorted, a mixture of hurt and anger flashing in his eyes. "Something you couldn't find here?" he echoed, his voice tinged with bitterness. "After everything we've built, everything we've shared... I'm not enough?"

She shook her head, the words catching in her throat. "It's not that," she said, struggling to explain the tangled mess of emotions inside her. "I just... I felt trapped, suffocated. I needed to feel alive again."

"Alive?" He laughed bitterly, shaking his head. "So, what, you found someone else to make you feel alive? You found someone else to give you what I can't?"

She flinched at the accusation, the truth of it piercing her, leaving her exposed. "Oliver, please..."

He leaned forward, his gaze fierce, unrelenting. "Who is he, Dahlia?"

She felt her heart stop, the question hanging in the air, heavy and damning. She looked away, unable to face the pain in his eyes, the raw betrayal etched across his face. "It doesn't matter," she whispered, her voice trembling. "It's over. It didn't mean anything."

"It didn't mean anything?" He scoffed, his tone filled with disbelief. "Do you think that makes it better? Do you think that makes this any easier?"

He stood, pacing the room, his hands running through his hair, frustration and hurt radiating from him. "I trusted you, Dahlia. I thought... I thought we had something real."

She felt the guilt press down on her, suffocating, but even as his words cut through her, the thought of Carlos lingered, a quiet, insistent hum that refused to be silenced. She had tasted freedom, passion, something that had made her feel alive in a way she hadn't felt in years, and now, the thought of letting it go, of returning to the life she had known, filled her with dread.

"I'm sorry," she whispered, the words hollow, meaningless in the face of his hurt.

He looked at her, his gaze hard, unyielding. "Sorry?" he repeated, his voice laced with bitterness. "That's all you have to say?"

He shook his head, his expression unreadable. "I deserve better than this, Dahlia. I deserve the truth."

She felt the walls closing in, the weight of her choices pressing down on her, but even as the guilt gnawed at her, she couldn't bring herself to regret the nights she had spent with Carlos, the life she had glimpsed in his arms. And in that moment, she realized that she wasn't ready to let it go.

"I can't... I can't do this anymore," she whispered, her voice barely audible. "I can't pretend that everything is okay, that I'm happy."

His face contorted with pain, a raw vulnerability flashing in his eyes. "Then maybe you should leave," he said, his voice cold, final.

Across town, Carlos was facing a confrontation of his own. Eve stood in the doorway, her arms crossed, her gaze fierce, unrelenting. She had been waiting for him, her expression a mix of anger and heartbreak that left him feeling exposed, vulnerable.

"Where were you, Carlos?" she asked, her voice steady, controlled, but laced with a quiet fury.

He hesitated, his mind scrambling for an answer, but he knew that the usual excuses, the carefully constructed lies, would crumble under her gaze. "Eve, I..."

She shook her head, her expression hardening. "Don't lie to me," she said, her voice cold, sharp. "I know about her."

The admission hit him like a punch, stealing the breath from his lungs. He could see the hurt in her eyes, the raw betrayal that he had caused, and for a moment, he felt the weight of his actions, the undeniable truth of the pain he had inflicted.

"How long?" she demanded, her voice barely above a whisper, but it held a strength that left him speechless. "How long have you been seeing her?"

He looked away, unable to meet her gaze, unable to face the hurt he had caused. "It... it just happened," he said, his voice soft, almost pleading. "I didn't mean for it to go this far. I was... I was lost, Eve. I needed something..."

"Something?" Her laugh was bitter, sharp, cutting through his excuses. "You needed something? And what about us, Carlos? What about our life, our family? Was that not enough?"

He felt the guilt settle over him, a crushing weight that left him breathless, but even as the regret gnawed at him, he couldn't deny the thrill he had found in Dahlia, the sense of freedom, of passion that had reignited a fire he hadn't known was missing.

"I'm sorry," he whispered, the words barely more than a breath, but even as he spoke them, he knew they were empty, hollow, a futile attempt to soothe a wound too deep to heal.

Eve's gaze softened, a flicker of vulnerability breaking through the anger. "Carlos," she murmured, her voice a quiet plea. "If there's any part of you that still loves me, that still wants this life... end it. End it now."

He felt a pang of desperation, a sudden, overwhelming sense of loss, but even as he looked at her, the memory of Dahlia lingered, a quiet, insistent hum that refused to be silenced. He knew, in that moment, that he was caught between two worlds, two lives that could not coexist.

"Eve, I..." He took a deep breath, forcing himself to meet her gaze. "I need time."

Her expression hardened, her gaze fierce, unyielding. "You don't have time, Carlos. Either you end it... or we're done."

Later that night, as Dahlia sat alone, her mind a whirlwind of guilt, fear, and a stubborn, unrelenting desire, she found herself thinking of Carlos. The confrontation with Oliver had shaken her, had left her feeling exposed, vulnerable, but even as the guilt gnawed at her, she couldn't deny the thrill, the undeniable pull she felt for Carlos.

But as she replayed the confrontation in her mind, the anger in Oliver's voice, the hurt in his eyes, she felt a chill settle over her, a quiet, insistent whisper that warned her of the danger, the risks she was taking. She knew, deep down, that she was treading on dangerous ground, that her life, her marriage, her very existence was teetering on the edge.

But even as the fear took root, she felt a surge of defiance, a fierce, unrelenting resolve that refused to be silenced. She wouldn't lose Carlos. She couldn't.

I won't let him leave me, she thought, a quiet, desperate determination settling over her. *He's mine, and I won't let him go.*

She remembered the stories her grandmother had told her, the quiet whispers of power, of rituals that could bind, could keep what was hers from slipping away. She had pushed those stories aside, buried them beneath the life she had built with Oliver, but now, as the weight of her choices bore down on her, as the reality of losing Carlos crept closer, she felt a quiet, desperate resolve take root within her.

Her grandmother had spoken of the spirits, of the power that resided in the old ways, the ways of their ancestors.

Dahlia had listened to those stories with awe as a child, wide-eyed and enraptured, her grandmother's voice a soothing murmur in the quiet night. Her grandmother had told her of rituals that could summon love, rituals that could make a man's heart belong to her alone, no matter who or what stood in the way.

"When you find love," her grandmother had whispered, her voice laced with a wisdom that had seemed both beautiful and dangerous, *"never let it go. And if it tries to leave you, bind it. Call upon the spirits. They will give you the power to keep what is yours."*

Dahlia had never thought she would need those words, had dismissed them as stories meant to scare or enchant a child. But now, as she sat alone in the darkness, her heart aching with the thought of losing Carlos, she found herself drawn to those memories, to the promise they held. She could almost hear her grandmother's voice, echoing through her mind like a quiet, steady drumbeat, a reminder that she held a power she had never claimed.

Her hands trembled as she reached for her phone, pulling up Carlos's name, her fingers hovering over the screen, hesitant yet filled with a fierce, unrelenting determination. She knew she was treading on dangerous ground, that what she was considering was a path that would change everything, that would bind her to Carlos in ways that could not be undone.

But as she thought of his hands on her skin, of the way he had made her feel alive, seen, cherished, she felt the doubt slip away, replaced by a certainty that left her breathless, a quiet, consuming fire that refused to be extinguished.

I won't let him go.

And as she sat there, the darkness wrapping around her like a cloak, she began to whisper the words her grandmother had taught her, the ancient incantations that would bind Carlos to her, that would make him hers, and hers alone. The words slipped from her lips, soft and steady, each one a quiet promise, a vow that echoed through the stillness, a declaration of a love that would not be denied.

By the time she finished, a sense of calm had settled over her, a quiet certainty that she was finally in control, that the life she had chosen was now hers to keep. She felt the power of the words, the weight of her choice, and she knew that this was only the beginning, that she had stepped into a world that was both dangerous and intoxicating.

And as she sat there, alone in the silence, she felt a quiet thrill, a sense of liberation that left her breathless, her heart racing with the knowledge that Carlos was now bound to her, that nothing would ever come between them again.

This was her love, her life, her destiny—and she would let nothing, and no one, stand in her way.

Chapter 7: Unseen Forces and Unleashed Obsession

The night was a canvas of shadows as Dahlia made her way to the clearing, the one she had visited in the past only for simple rituals—those she'd done out of curiosity and longing, yet none as powerful as the one she planned for tonight. Tonight was different. The air seemed thick, electric, humming with something ancient and ominous, as though the very spirits she sought to summon were already aware, awaiting her call.

The clearing was dark, swallowed by towering trees that loomed overhead like silent guardians. Only a sliver of the moonlight broke through the dense canopy, casting an eerie glow across the ground. Dahlia knelt down, her fingers trembling slightly as she pulled out the items she had gathered in secret. Her grandmother's warnings whispered in her mind, but she ignored them, brushing aside the memories like cobwebs as she laid out her materials.

She began with the candle—black, thick, its wax a gleaming shade that absorbed the light rather than reflected it. She placed it in the center of the clearing, lighting it carefully, the flame casting long, sinuous shadows around her. The scent of the smoke was pungent, bitter, and as it curled upward, she felt a shiver run down her spine. There was something different about this candle, something potent that set it apart from the mundane.

Next, she scattered a ring of herbs around the candle, each leaf and petal chosen carefully: belladonna for secrecy, mandrake for power, and dried henbane to heighten the intensity. Each handful of herbs seemed to pulse with energy as she dropped them, as if the earth itself recognized the dark purpose she was summoning. A fine powder of crushed bone and ash dusted the edges of the ring, the residue of something once living, something now bound to her will.

Then, the final element—a lock of her hair, bound tightly with black thread, and a vial of her own blood. She uncorked the vial, the metallic scent filling her nostrils as she held it over the flame, letting a single drop sizzle into the heat, its hiss rising like a serpent's whisper in the silence. She whispered her grandmother's words, each syllable falling from her lips in a language she didn't fully understand but felt in the depths of her soul. Her voice was low, reverent, the words a rhythmic chant that grew louder, more insistent, as she felt the power building around her.

"Spirits of the shadows, hear me. Spirits of the earth, heed my call. Let no one come between me and the one I claim. Remove her from his path, from his life, from his very soul."

Her voice was a crescendo, filling the night air, resonating with the dark energy that seemed to pulse from the earth itself. She felt the power swirling around her, wrapping her in a cocoon of darkness, as if the spirits themselves were reaching out, answering her call. The ground beneath her hands felt warm, alive, as though something ancient was stirring just beneath the surface, ready to rise at her command.

She continued the chant, her voice growing louder, more frenzied, as if the words had taken on a life of their own. Her hands trembled as she raised them, palms facing the sky, the black candle casting a flickering light over her face. Her gaze was fierce, her eyes reflecting the dark flame, her expression one of intensity, of power, as though she had been consumed by the very ritual she was performing.

And then she felt it—a surge of energy, dark and raw, rushing up from the ground, filling her with a force that was both terrifying and exhilarating. It coursed through her veins like fire, igniting every nerve, every sense, until she felt as though she were no longer bound to the earth but suspended between worlds, connected to something far beyond her understanding.

The shadows around her began to move, twisting and writhing as if alive, their dark forms stretching and coiling, filling the clearing with a pulsating energy that seemed to echo her heartbeat. The wind picked up, swirling around her, carrying her voice through the trees, the words spilling from her lips in a frenzied chant, a crescendo of dark promises.

"Remove her. Bind him to me. Let no one stand in my way. Let no one claim him but I."

The chant grew louder, each word a pulse that seemed to resonate through the very fabric of the night. The wind whipped around her, tearing at her hair, her clothes, the chill biting into her skin, but she was oblivious, lost in the power she had unleashed. Her body felt weightless, as though the energy of the ritual had lifted her from the ground, leaving her suspended in the air, her hands raised, her eyes closed as she gave herself over to the dark force that filled her.

And then, as the final word left her lips, the wind stopped. The shadows stilled, and an eerie silence fell over the clearing. Dahlia opened her eyes, her gaze falling on the black candle, the flame flickering weakly, as though struggling to survive the intensity of the ritual. She felt drained, every ounce of energy sapped from her, but within that exhaustion was a sense of triumph, a dark satisfaction that filled her with a quiet certainty.

The power she had summoned was real. She had felt it in her bones, in her blood, a force that had acknowledged her call and answered. And as she stood there, alone in the silence, she knew that Eve's days were numbered. The spirits would see to it. They would fulfill her desire, remove her obstacle, bind Carlos to her in a way that nothing—not even his marriage—could undo.

As she turned to leave, the shadows seemed to follow her, slipping through the trees, their dark forms a reminder of the power she had claimed, a power that now belonged to her.

In the days that followed, Dahlia felt a change within her. It was subtle at first, a quiet intensity that simmered beneath the surface, a sense of control that filled her with confidence. She moved through her daily routine with a newfound purpose, a certainty that had replaced the desperation she had once felt.

But the power came with a price. She began to experience visions, strange, fleeting images that flashed before her eyes—a dark figure standing in the shadows, a pair of eyes watching her from the darkness, the faint whisper of a voice that seemed to echo in her mind. At night, her dreams were filled with images of Eve, her face twisted in pain, her voice a pleading whisper that left Dahlia with a sense of unease she couldn't shake.

And then there were the signs. Small, unsettling occurrences that seemed to follow her wherever she went—a chill that settled over her when she was alone, a feeling of being watched, the flicker of shadows in the corner of her vision. She tried to brush it off as paranoia, a side effect of the ritual's intensity, but the feeling lingered, growing stronger with each passing day.

Carlos, too, began to feel the effects of the ritual. He was drawn to her with an intensity that bordered on obsession, his thoughts consumed by her, his every waking moment filled with the need to see her, to be with her. But there was something else, a sense of unease that settled over him whenever they were together, as though an invisible presence were watching them, a force that bound them together in a way he couldn't explain.

One evening, as they lay together, he looked at her, his gaze intense, searching. "Dahlia," he murmured, his voice soft, hesitant. "Have you ever... have you ever felt like we're not alone? Like there's something... something here with us?"

She looked at him, her expression unreadable, the memory of the ritual flashing in her mind. She knew what he was feeling, could sense the power that lingered between them, the force that had answered her call. But she smiled, reaching out to touch his face, her fingers tracing the line of his jaw.

"It's just us," she whispered, her voice a quiet assurance. "Only us."

But as she held him, a chill settled over her, a reminder of the power she had summoned, a force that would not be denied. The warmth between them felt hollow, something fragile and fleeting beneath the weight of what she'd called upon. The shadows in the room seemed to shift, stretching along the walls like fingers, grasping, claiming the space between them, a darkness that was no longer just in her mind.

Carlos shuddered, as though feeling it too. He closed his eyes, his breathing shallow, a faint tremor running through him that only intensified as the minutes slipped by. Dahlia tightened her grip, a wave of possessive protectiveness coursing through her, yet even as she held him, she could feel him slipping, as though something were tugging at his soul, fraying the connection that bound them together.

"Dahlia," he whispered, his voice barely audible, as if he were speaking to himself, lost in the labyrinth of his own mind. "There's something wrong... I can't... I feel like I'm drowning. Like... like I'm disappearing."

The words sent a shiver down her spine, cold and sharp, but she forced herself to smile, to reassure him. "You're not going anywhere, Carlos," she whispered, her voice steady but hollow, as though the room itself swallowed her words. "I'm here. You're with me. That's all that matters."

But even as she spoke, she felt a pulse, a deep, steady throb that echoed in her bones, reverberating through her chest, each beat a reminder of the ritual she had performed, the darkness she had summoned. The shadows in the room thickened, coiling around them, their tendrils reaching, slipping into every corner, every crevice, until the room felt stifling, suffocating.

Carlos pulled away, his face pale, his eyes wide with fear. "Do you feel that?" he whispered, his voice barely more than a breath. "There's... something here. I can't see it, but I can feel it. It's like... like something's watching us."

She forced a smile, reaching for his hand, but he pulled away, his gaze flickering toward the shadows, his breathing shallow, his face lined with dread.

"Dahlia," he said, his voice trembling. "What did you do?"

Her heart skipped, her mind flashing back to the ritual, to the promises she had made, the forces she had called upon, forces that were beyond her understanding, beyond her control. But she couldn't tell him the truth—not now, not when he was already slipping, already questioning.

"Carlos, there's nothing—"

A sudden gust of wind tore through the room, extinguishing the candles in an instant, plunging them into darkness. The air was thick, dense, pressing down on them with an intensity that left her gasping for breath. She could feel it, the presence that had answered her call, the force that now surrounded them, filling every inch of space with a weight that was both suffocating and intoxicating.

She reached out, her hand finding his in the darkness, but his grip was weak, trembling, as though he were barely holding on. His breathing was shallow, rapid, each inhale a struggle against the force that pressed down on them, binding them together, yet pushing them apart in the same breath.

A voice echoed in her mind, soft and insistent, a whisper that sent chills down her spine. *"You called us... we answered... but there is always a price."*

The words echoed, each syllable sinking into her mind, filling her with a sense of dread that settled in her bones, a weight that was both familiar and foreign, as though she had always known, deep down, that this moment would come. She clutched Carlos's hand, her fingers digging into his skin, but even as she held him, she could feel the darkness wrapping around them, binding them in ways she hadn't anticipated.

He gasped, his voice a strained whisper. "Dahlia... what did you do? I can feel it... I can feel it in my soul, like something's... pulling me apart."

She closed her eyes, willing herself to be calm, to ignore the fear that gnawed at her, but the voice in her mind grew louder, insistent, a reminder of the price she had agreed to pay, a price that was no longer hers to control.

"What you desire... will be yours... but all things come at a cost."

The words filled her mind, a haunting promise that resonated in the silence, leaving her breathless, her heart racing as the weight of her choices settled over her like a shroud. She opened her eyes, her gaze meeting his, and in that moment, she saw the fear, the vulnerability, the desperation that mirrored her own.

"Carlos," she whispered, her voice barely more than a breath. "I didn't... I didn't mean for this to happen."

He shook his head, his grip on her hand weakening as he pulled away, his gaze filled with something close to horror. "This... this isn't love, Dahlia," he said, his voice trembling, each word a knife that cut through her. "Whatever you did... it's consuming us. It's... it's not natural."

The words struck her, leaving her breathless, a raw ache settling in her chest, a reminder of the forces she had called upon, forces that now lingered, waiting, watching. She felt the darkness coil around her, a quiet reminder that her choices were no longer hers to undo, that the path she had chosen was one she could not abandon.

"What you desire will be yours..."

The words echoed, filling her with a sense of dread that was both intoxicating and terrifying. She had done this— had bound him to her, had called upon forces that now claimed him, body and soul. And even as she felt the horror of it, there was a part of her that reveled in the power, a part of her that relished the control, the knowledge that he was hers, bound to her in ways he could never escape.

But as she looked into his eyes, saw the fear, the pain, the realization that he was slipping away, a flicker of doubt crept in, a quiet whisper that warned her of the price that awaited, the cost that would not be denied.

Carlos stumbled back, his gaze darting to the shadows, his breathing shallow, his face lined with horror. "Dahlia... please... whatever you did, make it stop. I can't... I can't live like this."

She reached for him, her fingers trembling, but he pulled away, his gaze filled with a fear that mirrored her own, a fear that was no longer just for himself, but for her, for the darkness that now surrounded them, binding them together in ways she hadn't foreseen.

"I can't," she whispered, her voice filled with a desperation that mirrored his. "I don't know how..."

The words hung in the air, thick and heavy, a reminder of the choices she had made, choices that were no longer hers to control. And as the darkness closed in, as the weight of the ritual settled over them, she realized, with a chilling certainty, that this was only the beginning, that the forces she had called upon were only just beginning to reveal their true nature.

"There is always a price," the voice whispered, a haunting reminder that echoed in the silence, a promise of the darkness that awaited, a darkness that would consume them both, body and soul.

And as the night deepened, as the shadows coiled around them, Dahlia felt a chill settle over her, a reminder that she had unleashed something far beyond her understanding, something that would not be denied, something that would bind them together in ways she could never escape.

The darkness was coming, and it would not be stopped.

Chapter 8: Echoes of the Past

Dahlia's world felt like it was splintering. The night closed around her like a vice, pressing from every angle, and the silence felt different tonight—weighted, thick, almost tangible, as though it had settled in the air just to suffocate her. Her mind was a whirl of thoughts, fragments of memory, each one tearing at the edges of her mind, sharp and relentless. She had thought she could control it all, that her love for Carlos would make everything fall perfectly into place. She could practically hear her own words from earlier echoing in the room, her tone fierce and possessive, but now, in the silence, they rang hollow.

Carlos had looked at her with such anguish tonight, his voice haunted, the same quiet, desperate confession playing over and over in her mind: *"I don't know who I am anymore, Dahlia..."*

The way he had looked at her, his eyes searching hers as though he were lost in the very place he had come to for salvation, had left her feeling raw, exposed. For the first time, the strength she had always felt when she was near him, the confidence that had carried her through all the rituals and the risks, was gone. She felt only his absence, an absence that crept into the very corners of the room, settling over her, cold and unyielding. She tried to brush off the feeling, but it lingered, a quiet ache that throbbed in her chest.

The house was dark, the faint ticking of the clock in the hallway the only sound, marking each second as it slipped by, dragging her deeper into a silence that felt as though it might swallow her whole. She ran her fingers over the stem of the wine glass in her hand, her gaze fixed on the doorway where Carlos had stood just hours before. She tried to imagine him standing there again, the way he had so many times, his presence filling the space with warmth, but now it felt different. The doorway was empty, a shadowed frame that only emphasized his absence, and no matter how much she tried to will him back, the space remained hollow.

Desperation clawed at her, sharp and unforgiving. She stood abruptly, the wine sloshing in the glass, her movements tense, her mind buzzing with the need to escape the silence, to do something, anything, to fill the emptiness that now surrounded her. Her gaze flicked to the photograph on the wall, the one she hadn't looked at in what felt like years, but tonight it seemed to draw her in, as though it held some secret, some answer to the turmoil in her heart. She moved closer, her footsteps soft against the floor, her gaze fixed on the image.

It was a picture of her and Oliver, taken just after their wedding. She barely recognized the woman staring back at her—a woman whose eyes held a brightness, a warmth, a hope that felt like a distant memory. She looked young, foolish, innocent in a way that felt almost foreign, as though she were seeing a stranger, someone who belonged to another time, another life.

A pang of guilt rippled through her as she remembered how much Oliver had loved her, how he had tried to build a life with her, a life filled with dreams she had once shared but had since discarded. The memories of their early days together, filled with laughter and promises whispered late into the night, felt like fragments of a story she could barely remember. She had moved so far from that life, so far from the love she had once known, that it felt like a story she had read rather than lived. Yet, as she looked at the photo, she couldn't shake the feeling that there was something deeper, something more that she was missing.

The thought gnawed at her, an itch she couldn't scratch, a whisper at the edge of her consciousness that refused to be silenced. She turned away from the photo, the feeling of déjà vu settling over her like a blanket, a feeling so familiar it was almost painful. She couldn't shake the sense that she had been here before, standing in the same room, feeling the same emptiness, the same loss.

Her hand trembled as she set the glass down, her gaze drifting to the clock, watching the second hand as it ticked away, each second stretching out into an eternity. She felt as though she were caught in a loop, each moment folding into the next, dragging her back to a place she had tried to leave behind, a place filled with shadows and whispers that haunted her every step.

A sudden, desperate need for answers gripped her, pulling her from the house, her feet carrying her through the darkened streets, past the rows of quiet, sleeping houses, each one casting long shadows that seemed to reach out to her, as though they were alive, as though they knew her secrets. She barely registered her surroundings, her mind consumed by thoughts of Carlos, by the memory of his touch, his voice, the way he had looked at her tonight, lost and adrift, searching for something he couldn't find.

The night air was cool against her skin, each step grounding her, but only barely. She found herself drawn toward his house, her movements slow, deliberate, as though she were walking through water, each step heavy with the weight of her own desperation. She didn't know what she hoped to find or if he'd even be there, but the pull was irresistible, a force that felt both familiar and foreign, like an echo of something she had known once but had since forgotten.

As she approached his house, she slowed, her gaze fixed on the dimly lit windows, searching for any sign of him. The street was silent, the only sound the faint hum of her own breath as she crept closer, hiding in the shadows, her heart pounding with a mix of hope and dread. She could see a light on in one of the upstairs windows, a warm, inviting glow that cut through the darkness.

Without thinking, she moved closer, her footsteps light, her breath barely more than a whisper as she reached the edge of his driveway, hidden from view. She looked up, her gaze fixed on the window, the light casting a faint silhouette against the curtain, and then she saw him.

Carlos stepped into view, his face pale, his eyes dark with exhaustion, but his expression... his expression was one she didn't recognize. He looked like a stranger, his gaze distant, hollow, as though he were seeing something she couldn't, as though he were trapped in a world she couldn't reach.

He was speaking, his lips moving, but she couldn't hear the words, only the cadence, the soft, pleading tone that hinted at a conversation filled with desperation. And then another figure joined him, a woman's form, her features obscured by the curtain, but Dahlia knew, with a certainty that cut through her, that it was Eve.

Eve's hand rested on his shoulder, her touch gentle, grounding, as though she were pulling him back from the edge of something dark, something unknown. The sight filled Dahlia with a surge of anger, a flash of jealousy so intense it left her breathless, her hands clenched at her sides. How dare she—how dare Eve think she could still hold onto him, after everything?

But even as the anger surged, a quiet sense of dread settled over her, a realization that this moment, this scene, was all too familiar, as though she had stood here before, watched this same conversation unfold, felt this same burning ache of loss. It was as if the past were folding in on itself, merging with the present, dragging her back to a place she didn't want to go.

She stepped back, her heart racing, her mind spinning as fragments of memory flooded her senses. She could see herself standing here, in this very spot, consumed by the same anger, the same desperation, but the images were fragmented, slipping through her fingers like sand. She turned, stumbling back to the car, her pulse pounding, her mind filled with questions she couldn't answer, memories that didn't belong to her but felt as real as her own skin.

By the time she reached her house, she was trembling, her body exhausted from the weight of the memories, the realization that had begun to settle over her like a shroud. She stumbled inside, her hands shaking as she closed the door, her gaze drifting to the empty room, the silence pressing down on her, filling every corner, every shadow with a sense of loss, of something unfinished.

She moved through the house, her steps slow, her mind a whirlwind of emotions, her gaze flickering to the objects around her, each one a reminder of a life she had tried to leave behind, a life she couldn't escape. The clock on the wall ticked away, each second dragging her back, back to the beginning, back to a place she had been before, a place she was bound to return to, again and again.

In the quiet, in the solitude, she felt the weight of her curse, the loop that had bound her, the cycle that had brought her back to the same place, time and time again, each life a mirror of the last, each love a reflection of the one before. She sank to the floor, her gaze fixed on the empty room, the silence pressing down on her, a silence filled with the echoes of her past, the memories of lives lost, loves unfulfilled, a curse that bound her, body and soul, to a life that would never be hers.

and as the night stretched on, as the darkness settled around her like a cloak, she felt the weight of the loop pressing down, an invisible chain, binding her to a destiny that felt both familiar and foreign. Her hands clenched, fingers digging into the cold floor, grounding her, as she tried to steady her breathing, to calm the whirlwind of emotions that raged within her.

The silence grew thicker, almost tangible, wrapping around her like a shroud. Her mind drifted back, her thoughts slipping into fragments of memory, images flashing before her eyes—a different room, a different time, a different face. She saw herself standing in the same position, her hands clenched, her heart heavy with the same sense of loss, the same desperation that filled her now.

She closed her eyes, letting the memories wash over her, feeling them slip through her fingers like water, each one a reminder of the lives she had lived, the loves she had lost, the dreams that had slipped through her grasp. She could feel the weight of each one, pressing down on her, a reminder of the price she had paid, the sacrifices she had made, only to find herself back here, in the same place, bound by the same curse.

The memories were like a storm, swirling around her, each one a fragment of a life she could barely remember, a life she had tried to escape, only to be pulled back, again and again, to the same beginning, the same love, the same loss. She felt as though she were drowning, suffocating beneath the weight of her own memories, each one a reminder of the love she had tried to hold onto, only to lose it, time and time again.

Her mind drifted to Carlos, to the way he had looked at her tonight, his gaze filled with confusion, with fear, as though he were slipping away from her, as though he could sense the darkness that bound them together, the shadows that lingered in the corners of her mind, waiting to claim him, as they had claimed so many others.

She felt a surge of desperation, a need to hold onto him, to keep him close, to make him hers, in a way that no one else ever had. She reached out, her fingers tracing the cold floor, as though she could reach out to him, hold him, keep him from slipping away. But even as she reached, she could feel him slipping, slipping through her fingers, like sand, like water, like every other love she had tried to claim, only to find herself back in the same place, bound by the same curse.

And in that moment, she felt a surge of anger, a fierce, unrelenting rage, that filled her with a sense of power, of control. She would not lose him, not this time. She would find a way to break the curse, to escape the loop that bound her, to make him hers, in a way that no one else ever had.

Her mind drifted back to the ritual, to the power she had summoned, the darkness she had called upon, in her desperate attempt to bind him to her, to make him hers, in a way that no one else ever could. She could feel the power lingering, a quiet, insistent hum that filled the air around her, a reminder of the forces she had unleashed, forces that waited, watching, waiting to claim their due.

She took a deep breath, steadying herself, as she rose to her feet, her gaze fixed on the shadows that lingered in the corners of the room, shadows that seemed to pulse with a life of their own, shadows that watched her, waiting, a reminder of the price she had paid, the sacrifices she had made, in her desperate attempt to claim a love that was never hers to keep.

And as she stood there, in the silence, in the darkness, she felt a quiet, unrelenting resolve settle over her. She would not lose him, not this time. She would find a way to break the curse, to escape the loop that bound her, to claim the love that had eluded her for so long.

The shadows shifted, pulsing, as though in response to her thoughts, a quiet, insistent reminder of the forces that waited, watching, waiting to claim their due. But she ignored them, her gaze fixed on the empty space before her, a space that she would fill, a love that she would claim, no matter the cost.

She moved through the house, her steps slow, deliberate, as though she were moving through water, each step heavy with the weight of her own resolve. She would find a way to break the curse, to escape the loop that bound her, to make him hers, in a way that no one else ever had.

Chapter 9: The Breaking Point

Dahlia felt the walls closing in. She could still feel the strange energy from her last ritual, the one she had used to try and keep Carlos bound to her, reverberating through her mind. Every corner of her house felt charged, almost alive, as though the shadows themselves held secrets she couldn't understand. Her thoughts spun in circles, each one leading back to the same question: *Why does it feel like I've been here before?*

She hadn't slept in days. She had been afraid to close her eyes, afraid of what she might see, what memories or visions might come creeping in if she allowed herself even a moment of peace. Her skin felt too tight, her heart racing as though she were running out of time, her very breath coming in shallow gasps. She tried to hold onto the certainty that had guided her through every ritual, every desperate act to make Carlos hers, but even that felt like it was slipping away.

When a knock came at her door, sharp and insistent, she jumped, the sound breaking through the silence like a gunshot. She didn't need to guess who it was—she knew. She felt him through the walls, sensed his fear, his desperation. Carlos.

She opened the door, her gaze meeting his, and for a moment, time seemed to stop. He looked different, as though he had aged in the span of a few days, his face lined with exhaustion, his eyes filled with something she couldn't quite read. He was afraid—no, terrified. But there was something else in his gaze, something darker, more resolute.

"Dahlia," he whispered, his voice barely more than a breath, as though saying her name hurt. "We need to talk."

The silence between them felt like a living thing, heavy and unyielding, pressing down on her, filling the space with a tension she could almost taste. She stepped back, allowing him inside, her heart pounding as she watched him move through the doorway, his steps hesitant, as though he were crossing a threshold he could never return from.

"What's going on, Carlos?" she asked, her voice soft, a whisper that barely broke the silence.

He looked at her, his gaze searching, as though he were seeing her for the first time, his eyes filled with a mixture of fear and desperation that sent a shiver down her spine. "I don't know how to say this," he murmured, his voice trembling. "But... I feel like I've been here before. Like I've... lived this life, this moment, over and over."

The words hit her like a blow, leaving her breathless, her heart pounding as she tried to process what he was saying. She had felt it too, the strange sense of familiarity, the feeling that each moment was a shadow of something that had already happened, but she had pushed it aside, convinced it was just her mind playing tricks. But hearing him say it, hearing the fear in his voice, made it real.

"Carlos," she whispered, her voice trembling. "I don't know what you're talking about."

But even as she spoke, the words felt hollow, empty, a lie she could barely believe herself. She knew, deep down, that there was something more, something lurking in the shadows of her own mind, waiting to be uncovered.

Carlos took a step closer, his gaze intense, his face lined with desperation. "I see you in my dreams, Dahlia," he murmured, his voice barely more than a breath. "But it's not... it's not just dreams. It's memories. Memories of lives I've lived, lives we've lived. But each time... it ends the same way."

A chill settled over her, a coldness that seeped into her bones, leaving her feeling as though she were standing on the edge of an abyss, staring into a darkness that had no end. She opened her mouth to speak, to deny his words, but the truth clawed its way to the surface, filling her with a terror she couldn't ignore.

"I don't understand," she whispered, her voice trembling, her gaze fixed on him, searching his face for any hint of familiarity, any clue that would explain the feeling that had haunted her for as long as she could remember.

"Why does it feel like... like this has all happened before?"

He looked away, his hands clenching at his sides, his shoulders tense, as though he were bracing himself for a truth that would destroy them both. "Because it has," he murmured, his voice barely audible. "We're... trapped, Dahlia. Trapped in a loop, a cycle that never ends."

The words hung in the air, heavy and unyielding, a weight that pressed down on her, filling her with a sense of dread that left her breathless. She could feel the truth of his words, a truth that resonated deep within her, as though her very soul recognized the pattern, the unbreakable loop that bound them together.

"No," she whispered, her voice barely more than a breath, her heart pounding as she fought against the realization that was clawing its way to the surface. "No, that can't be true. We're not... we're not trapped."

Carlos looked at her, his gaze filled with a sorrow that cut through her, leaving her feeling hollow, empty, as though a part of her had been ripped away. "We are, Dahlia," he said, his voice soft, a quiet acceptance that left her breathless. "I don't know how, or why, but every time... every time, it ends the same way. I try to leave, but something pulls me back. I can feel it... in my soul."

The room seemed to close in around her, the walls pressing down, the shadows growing darker, more suffocating, as the truth settled over her, a truth she couldn't ignore. She had felt it too, the sense of inevitability, the feeling that no matter how hard she tried, she would always end up back here, trapped in the same story, the same love, the same loss.

"No," she murmured, her voice trembling, her gaze fixed on the floor as she tried to hold onto the fragments of her own resolve, the belief that she could change it, that she could make him hers, once and for all. "I won't... I won't let it end this way. Not this time."

Carlos took a step back, his expression wary, his gaze filled with a fear that cut through her, leaving her feeling exposed, vulnerable, as though he could see into the darkest corners of her soul. "What are you going to do, Dahlia?" he asked, his voice a quiet challenge, a dare that left her breathless, her heart pounding.

She looked at him, her gaze fierce, her jaw set, her determination unwavering. "Whatever it takes," she whispered, her voice steady, a promise that filled the room with a chilling intensity. "I'll do whatever it takes to keep you, Carlos."

But even as she spoke, a flicker of doubt crept into her mind, a quiet whisper that warned her of the darkness she was about to unleash, the forces she was about to call upon, forces that had claimed her once, and would not hesitate to claim her again.

Carlos took another step back, his gaze filled with a fear that mirrored her own, a fear that left her feeling as though she were standing on the edge of a cliff, staring into the abyss of her own soul. "I won't... I won't be part of this, Dahlia," he said, his voice trembling, his gaze fixed on her, as though he were searching for any hint of the woman he had once loved, the woman he had thought he knew.

A bitter smile twisted her lips, her heart heavy with the weight of the truth she had fought so hard to deny. "You don't have a choice," she murmured, her voice barely more than a breath, a whisper that filled the silence with a chilling finality. "You're mine, Carlos. You've always been mine."

The words hung in the air, a promise, a curse, a truth that bound them together, a truth that left her feeling both powerful and powerless, as though she were standing on the edge of her own destruction, and there was no turning back.

She took a step forward, her gaze fierce, her determination unwavering, as she reached for him, her hand closing around his, her grip tight, unyielding. "This time," she whispered, her voice filled with a fierce, unrelenting resolve, "I'll make sure nothing comes between us."

But as she spoke, a shadow flickered at the edge of her vision, a reminder of the forces she had called upon, the forces that had claimed her once, and were waiting, watching, ready to claim her again.

And in that moment, as the darkness closed in, as the shadows grew thicker, more suffocating, she felt the weight of her own actions, the price she had paid, the price she was about to pay again.

Chapter 10: Bound to Darkness

The night was thick with silence as Dahlia paced the room, her hands trembling, thoughts scattered, each one racing faster than the last. She could feel something slipping away, like grains of sand slipping through her fingers, each one a heartbeat, each one an echo of something she couldn't quite place. The house seemed to press down on her, shadows stretching longer, darker, almost alive, as though they were watching her, waiting for something to unfold.

Carlos was out there, somewhere. She could feel his presence like a faint pulse in the back of her mind, the warmth of his essence lingering even across the distance that separated them. But she knew—she felt it in her bones—that he was slipping away, as though the very air between them were stretching thin, ready to snap. She had felt it in his gaze earlier, the hesitation, the doubt. The need for her, for whatever power she held over him, had grown faint, like a whisper fading into silence.

Desperation clawed at her, sharp and unforgiving. She stood in the center of her living room, her heart pounding, as she reached for her grandmother's book, its pages worn, each one filled with rituals she'd studied for hours, night after night, memorizing every line, every symbol. She had called upon its power before, but tonight was different. Tonight, she would use the darkest spell she knew—a spell meant not just to bind but to claim, to take possession of his soul in a way that could never be undone.

Her fingers trembled as she turned to the page, her gaze settling on the symbols etched there, each one a promise, a price, a warning she could almost feel whispering beneath her skin. She laid out her materials in a circle: a black candle, thick and heavy, a lock of Carlos's hair she had carefully saved, a ring he'd once left behind without realizing. Each item pulsed with significance, a reminder of him, of the ties she had to him that felt as fragile as glass.

She knelt, arranging the items with care, her hands steady despite the tremor that ran through her veins. She lit the candle, the flame flickering as if uncertain, casting a faint glow that barely cut through the darkness. The air was thick, heavy, and she felt as though she were suffocating, as though the shadows were pressing in around her, wrapping her in their cold embrace.

Her voice was low, steady, a quiet chant that filled the room, each word resonating in the silence, vibrating with a power that she could feel coursing through her veins. She spoke the words slowly, each syllable precise, her focus unbreakable.

"Spirits of the shadows, spirits of the earth, I call upon you. Bind him to me, bind his soul, his heart, his mind. Let no one come between us. Let no force, no curse, no life or death part us. Make him mine, now and forever."

As she chanted, she felt the air shift, the room growing colder, a chill that seeped into her bones, into her soul, leaving her feeling hollow and empty, a vessel waiting to be filled. She closed her eyes, her mind filled with the image of Carlos, his face pale, his eyes dark with fear, with confusion, with a longing that mirrored her own. She could feel him, even now, his presence a warm, steady pulse that called to her, that filled her with a sense of peace, a sense of purpose.

But as the words left her lips, she felt something shift, a darkness seeping into her mind, filling her with memories that didn't feel like hers, images that felt both familiar and foreign, as though they were pieces of a life she had lived but could not remember.

She saw herself in a room, walls lined with shadows, a man's face half-hidden in the darkness, his eyes filled with fear, with sorrow, his voice a whisper, a plea. "Dahlia, please... let me go."

The image flickered, blurring, replaced by another and then another, each one a fragment, a life she had tried to leave behind, a life she could not escape. She saw herself standing over a man, her hand reaching out, fingers tracing the line of his jaw, her voice a soft whisper. "You're mine," she murmured, her voice filled with a fierce, unrelenting determination, a hunger that bordered on desperation.

Each image was a story, a memory, a love that had ended the same way, in shadows, in silence, in a love that had been claimed only to slip through her fingers, leaving her alone. The flame of the black candle pulsed, casting shadows that twisted and contorted along the walls as though they held their own secrets, their own desires, whispering truths she couldn't hear.

Her voice faltered, the chant she'd been reciting falling silent as a sense of dread settled over her. She could feel it in her bones, an ache, a pull that tugged at the deepest part of her soul, as though something within her recognized the ritual she was performing, the words she was speaking. Her grandmother's warnings echoed in her mind, the whispered caution she had heard as a child, words she had ignored in her desperation.

The fear that had been simmering beneath her determination began to bubble to the surface, her hands shaking as she stared down at the flickering flame, the light casting her face in sharp relief. She closed her eyes, her heart pounding, her breaths shallow as she tried to push the fear away, to focus on the only thing that mattered.

Carlos. He would be hers.

She gritted her teeth, her resolve hardening, the words spilling from her lips once more, fierce, relentless, a chant that filled the room with a dark, unyielding power. *"Bind him to me. Let him be mine, his soul, his heart, his mind, bound to me for eternity. Let no one come between us. Let no force, no life, no death part us."*

But as she spoke, as her voice echoed in the silence, she felt the darkness shift, the shadows pressing closer, filling the room with a sense of dread that sent a shiver down her spine. Her mind filled with images, fragments of memories that flickered in and out, each one a reminder of the lives she had lived, the loves she had lost, the promises she had made and broken, each one a thread in the tapestry of her curse.

She saw herself standing in a circle, much like this one, her hands covered in blood, her face pale, her eyes hollow, a shell of the woman she had once been. She could feel the weight of her actions, the price she had paid, the lives she had taken, all for the same thing, the same desire, the same love that had eluded her time and time again.

And then she saw him—Carlos. His face was clear, his eyes dark, filled with sorrow, with fear, with a longing that cut through her, leaving her breathless, her heart pounding as she reached for him, her fingers brushing his face, his skin warm beneath her touch. But even as she held him, she could feel him slipping, slipping through her fingers like sand, like water, like every other love she had tried to claim.

Her breath came in shallow gasps, her heart racing as she looked down at her hands, seeing the faint glow of the candlelight dancing across her skin, a reminder of the power she had claimed, the darkness she had embraced, the price she was willing to pay to keep him, to make him hers.

And in that moment, as she stood there, the weight of the ritual pressing down on her, the shadows growing darker, colder, she felt a flicker of doubt, a quiet whisper that warned her of the darkness she was about to unleash, the forces she was about to call upon, forces that had claimed her once and would not hesitate to claim her again.

The air was thick with tension, a suffocating weight that pressed down on her, filling her with a sense of dread that left her breathless, her mind filled with questions she could not answer. But even as the fear settled over her, as the weight of the ritual pressed down, she felt a fierce, unrelenting resolve, a hunger that bordered on madness, a desire that filled her with a sense of purpose, a purpose that was stronger than any fear, any doubt, any curse.

And as she stood there, her gaze fixed on the flickering flame, she spoke the final words, her voice a whisper, a promise that filled the room, a promise that bound them together, a promise that would never let them go.

"You are mine, Carlos. You will always be mine."

The candle flickered, the shadows twisting along the walls, stretching, reaching, as though they, too, were bound to her will, as though they, too, had answered her call. She could feel it, the weight of the power she had summoned, the darkness that filled the room, a darkness that seeped into her soul, binding her to him, binding him to her, in a love that would never end, in a curse that would never break.

And as the silence settled around her, heavy, unyielding, she knew that she had crossed a line, a line she could never return from, a line that bound her to him in a way that went beyond life, beyond death, beyond time itself.

In the darkness, in the silence, she knew that she was his, and he was hers.

Forever.

Chapter 11: Shadows Unbound

Carlos woke in a cold sweat, his heart thudding like a trapped bird against his ribs, his breaths shallow and ragged. The room felt wrong—smaller, darker, as if the shadows themselves were alive, watching him with an intensity that pressed against his skin. He sat up, feeling disoriented, his hands grasping the edge of the bed as though grounding himself could chase away the images that clung to his mind. His pulse raced, and in the silence, he could almost hear it: her voice, calling to him, soft, insistent, as though she were right beside him.

Dahlia.

He squeezed his eyes shut, her face flashing behind his eyelids, her dark, intense gaze a magnetic force he couldn't resist. Her name was a whisper in his mind, a pulse in his veins that refused to let go. Desperate, he tried to clear his mind, to shake her hold on him, but he could feel her presence creeping back, wrapping around him like an unseen force that reached into his very soul.

His phone buzzed on the bedside table, the screen glowing dimly in the dark. He reached for it, his heart catching as he saw her name.

The message was simple: *I need to see you.*

Carlos's fingers hovered over the screen, his instincts screaming for him to ignore it, to stay away, but his body was already moving. He dressed in a daze, his movements automatic, his mind torn between the urge to flee and the pull that drew him to her, stronger than reason, stronger than anything he could fight. He was out the door before he could talk himself out of it, the cool morning air biting against his skin as he drove, his knuckles white on the steering wheel, his mind racing with questions he couldn't answer.

When he arrived at Dahlia's house, he hesitated, his hand gripping the door handle as he stared at the familiar building. Every instinct told him to turn back, to leave, to run, but he couldn't move. She had a hold on him, a force that went beyond logic, beyond reason. With a deep breath, he forced himself out of the car, his footsteps heavy as he approached the door.

Dahlia was waiting for him, her silhouette framed in the dim light as she opened the door, her gaze intense, searching. There was a softness in her eyes, a vulnerability that drew him in, but beneath it, he sensed something darker, something that sent a chill down his spine.

"Carlos," she murmured, her voice low, filled with an emotion he couldn't name. She stepped aside, allowing him in, her hand brushing his arm as he passed. The touch sent a jolt through him, his senses heightening, his skin tingling where her fingers had lingered. He clenched his fists, trying to steady himself, but the sensation only grew stronger, her presence filling the room, wrapping around him, making it hard to breathe.

"What... what's going on, Dahlia?" he managed, his voice barely more than a whisper. He turned to face her, his gaze searching hers, trying to find the answers he couldn't articulate.

She looked at him for a long moment, her expression unreadable, her dark eyes holding a depth that left him feeling exposed, vulnerable, as though she could see into the very core of him. "You feel it too, don't you?" she asked softly, taking a step closer, her gaze never leaving his.

Carlos swallowed, his throat dry, the words catching in his throat. "I... I don't know what I feel. But it's... it's like I'm losing myself, like..." He paused, his voice trembling. "Like you're in my head, all the time. I can't... I can't get you out."

Dahlia's lips curved into a small, sad smile, her eyes filled with a longing that made his heart ache. "I know," she whispered, reaching out to touch his face, her fingers warm against his skin. "It's because we're connected, Carlos. In a way that goes beyond anything you can understand. We're bound together, by something stronger than fate."

He closed his eyes, her touch both comforting and suffocating, filling him with a sense of belonging that terrified him. "I don't... I don't want this, Dahlia," he said, his voice barely audible, his heart pounding as he forced himself to speak the words that had been clawing at him. "I feel like I'm... losing myself. Like I'm not... me anymore."

Her hand fell away, and he opened his eyes to find her watching him, her gaze filled with a pain that mirrored his own. "You are yourself, Carlos," she said quietly, her voice steady, though he could hear the tremor beneath it. "But you're also mine. We're bound together, by something deeper than either of us can control. It's not something you can just... walk away from."

He shook his head, backing away from her, his hands clenched at his sides. "This isn't love, Dahlia. This is... it's something else. Something dark. I don't even know who I am when I'm with you anymore."

Dahlia's eyes darkened, a flash of anger crossing her face. "You don't understand, Carlos," she said, her voice low, her gaze intense. "This is what we were meant for. You and I... we're part of something bigger, something that goes beyond this life."

He looked at her, the woman he had once thought he loved, now a stranger, a force he couldn't escape. "I don't want this," he said, his voice shaking. "I want my life back."

For a moment, she was silent, her gaze hardening as she studied him, as though she were seeing him for the first time. And then, her expression softened, a hint of sadness flickering in her eyes. "You think you have a choice?" she whispered, stepping closer, her voice barely more than a breath. "You think you can walk away, that you can just... go back to the life you had?"

He opened his mouth to respond, but she raised a finger, silencing him. "It's too late, Carlos. We're bound. I've made sure of it. You're mine now, in this life and every life after."

The words hit him like a blow, leaving him breathless, his mind racing as he struggled to comprehend what she was saying. "What... what do you mean?" he asked, his voice trembling.

Dahlia smiled, a bittersweet smile that sent a chill down his spine. "I bound you to me, Carlos," she said softly. "Through a ritual. Something... ancient. Something my family has known for generations." She paused, her gaze flickering to the book on the table, the one with pages yellowed from age, filled with symbols that seemed to pulse in the candlelight. "You're a part of me now. And no matter how much you fight it, no matter how much you try to deny it, that bond is stronger than anything you've ever known."

He stared at her, his mind reeling, the weight of her words pressing down on him like a stone. "You... you did this to me?" he whispered, his voice filled with disbelief, with horror. "You took away my life, my choices, and for what? To keep me here, trapped with you?"

Dahlia's gaze softened, her hand reaching for his, but he pulled back, his body tense, his heart pounding as he backed away. "No," he said, his voice barely more than a breath. "I don't want this. I don't want you."

Her face fell, her eyes darkening as his words cut through her. For a moment, he saw a flicker of pain, of vulnerability, and he almost reached out, almost let himself soften. But then her gaze hardened, her expression twisting with a resolve that sent a shiver through him.

"You don't understand, Carlos," she said, her voice steady, unwavering. "This isn't just about want. This is about destiny, about something that goes beyond either of us." She took a step closer, her gaze fierce, unyielding. "You may think you don't want this, but deep down, you know it's the truth. We're meant to be together. And there's nothing you or anyone else can do to change that."

He shook his head, backing toward the door, his mind racing, his heart pounding as he struggled to find a way out, a way to escape. "I don't care about destiny, or fate, or... or any of this!" he said, his voice rising. "I just want my life back, Dahlia. I want to be free."

She looked at him, her gaze intense, her voice a whisper filled with a quiet, haunting resolve. "There is no freedom, Carlos. Not from this. Not from me."

And in that moment, he felt it, the weight of her words settling over him, a chain that wrapped around his soul, binding him to her, to a fate he could not escape. He stared at her, his heart pounding, his breath coming in shallow gasps as he realized the truth—that there was no going back, no way out. She had claimed him, body and soul, bound him to a to a destiny he had never chosen, a future that felt as inevitable as it was terrifying. The shadows seemed to close in around him, the room growing smaller, tighter, as though the very air was conspiring to trap him within her grasp.

He felt the weight of her gaze, heavy, unyielding, as though her very soul had latched onto his, refusing to let go. There was a strange sadness in her eyes, a longing that flickered behind the fierce resolve, and for a brief moment, he saw the woman he had fallen in love with, the woman who had once felt so real, so full of warmth and light.

"Dahlia... please..." he whispered, his voice thick with desperation, his hands clenched at his sides as he struggled to hold onto the fragments of his own identity, to keep himself from slipping away entirely. "Let me go. Let us... let us find another way. This can't be what you want."

But Dahlia shook her head, her gaze hardening, her expression one of quiet determination that left no room for compromise. "You don't understand, Carlos," she said softly, her voice laced with a sorrow that sent a chill down his spine. "There is no other way. This is who we are. This is who I am. And you... you're part of me now, forever."

He backed away, his heart pounding, his mind racing as he searched for an escape, a way to break free from the web she had woven around him. But as he looked at her, saw the unbreakable resolve in her gaze, he realized, with a sinking dread, that there was no escape, that he was bound to her in ways he could not understand, in ways that went beyond reason, beyond love, beyond life itself.

And as the silence settled around them, heavy and unyielding, he felt the weight of the truth pressing down on him, a truth that left him breathless, that left him feeling as though he were standing on the edge of an abyss, staring into the darkness that had become his fate.

Chapter 12: A Vision of the Past

Dahlia stumbled down the dim hallway, her heartbeat drumming in her ears, each step heavier than the last. Shadows clung to her vision, distorting the edges of reality, pulling her toward something both familiar and terrifying. She could feel it—a presence lurking at the edges of her mind, a force she couldn't explain, couldn't ignore. The events of the last few days had left her frayed, each nerve stretched thin, her senses heightened to a breaking point. And now, as she moved forward, the world around her seemed to shift, as though bending to some hidden, irresistible force.

She took a deep breath, trying to steady herself, but the scent that filled her lungs wasn't the faint, stale air of her apartment. Instead, it was a rich blend of tobacco and roasted coffee beans, an earthy, comforting aroma that tugged at her memory with an aching familiarity. The smell was so vivid, so real, that she felt herself being pulled back in time, back to a place she had long since left behind.

"Dahlia..."

The whisper was soft, barely more than a breath, yet it echoed around her, filling the silence, weaving through her thoughts like a thread she couldn't grasp. She blinked, and suddenly, she was no longer in her apartment. The hallway around her had blurred and shifted, and she was standing instead in her grandmother's small, sunlit kitchen. The room felt warm, welcoming, with wooden beams overhead and sunlight streaming through a narrow window. Her gaze dropped to her feet, where she now wore the simple, worn sandals of her youth, and she saw herself dressed in the long skirt and linen blouse she'd worn as a young woman in Haiti.

A figure stood in the doorway, watching her with a quiet, unyielding intensity. Dahlia's heart clenched as recognition struck—a face lined with age, wise eyes as dark as onyx, filled with a knowing gaze that saw far beyond the present. It was her grandmother, a woman she had not seen in years, a woman whose memory was carved into the deepest parts of her heart. Yet here she was, looking as real, as alive, as she had all those years ago, her presence both comforting and unnerving.

"Granmé?" Dahlia's voice was a tremble, a whisper that barely broke the silence. She took a step forward, reaching out instinctively, her hands aching to touch, to feel, to anchor herself in the familiar warmth of her grandmother's embrace. But her grandmother's face remained stern, her expression guarded, unreadable as she looked at Dahlia with an intensity that made her chest tighten.

"You have returned," her grandmother murmured, her voice filled with a sorrow that cut through Dahlia, a sorrow that felt like a weight, heavy and unyielding. "But it is too late, chérie, isn't it?"

Dahlia shook her head, her pulse quickening as she took another step forward, her heart pounding in her chest. "Granmé, I don't understand," she whispered, her voice barely more than a breath, a plea. "Why are you here? Why am I... why am I seeing this?"

Her grandmother's gaze softened, a flicker of sadness crossing her face as she stepped closer, her hand reaching out to brush a strand of hair from Dahlia's face. The touch was real, warm, familiar, grounding her, even as she felt herself drifting in the dreamlike haze of the moment.

"I warned you, my sweet," her grandmother said softly, her voice filled with a sorrow that made Dahlia's heart ache, that made her want to turn away from the truth she saw reflected in those wise, unwavering eyes. "I told you that love would not come easily for you, that you were bound to something greater, something darker than you could ever understand."

Dahlia's mind raced, fragments of memories flashing before her eyes, moments she had tried to forget, moments that had haunted her in her dreams, leaving her feeling lost, adrift, searching for something she could never grasp. "I thought... I thought I could escape it," she murmured, her voice trembling. "I thought I could leave, that I could find love on my own terms, that I could... that I could be free."

Her grandmother's expression hardened, her gaze sharp and unyielding as she looked at Dahlia, as though seeing into the very core of her, seeing the choices she had made, the path she had taken. "You cannot escape what is written in the stars, Dahlia," she murmured, her voice a quiet, unbreakable truth. "You were born under a shadow, bound to a love that would find you and leave you, time and time again. That is the curse, my child. That is your fate."

The room seemed to shift, the walls blurring and distorting, the light flickering as Dahlia felt the weight of her grandmother's words settle over her, filling her with a dread that left her breathless, her heart pounding as she tried to fight against the truth, tried to hold onto the fragments of her own hope, her own dreams. "No," she whispered, her voice barely audible, her gaze fixed on the floor as she shook her head, as she tried to deny the truth that threatened to consume her. "That... that can't be true. I don't... I don't believe it."

But her grandmother's gaze remained steady, unwavering, filled with a knowledge that left no room for denial, no room for escape. "You may fight it, Dahlia. You may resist it, but the curse will find you, no matter where you go, no matter how far you run. It is woven into your soul, into the very fabric of your being. You are bound to it, and it is bound to you."

Dahlia felt a chill seep into her bones, an icy dread that left her feeling as though she were standing on the edge of an abyss, staring into a darkness that had no end. She could feel the memories flooding her mind, memories of Oliver, of the life she had left behind, of the choices she had made, each one a thread in the tapestry of her fate, each one leading her back to this moment, back to the truth she had tried so desperately to escape.

She saw herself as a young woman, standing in this very room, her heart filled with hope, with dreams of a life beyond the mountains, beyond the sea, a life where she could be free, where she could find love on her own terms. But her grandmother's words had been a shadow, a warning that had lingered, waiting to claim her, waiting to remind her of the price she would pay for her freedom.

"You are doomed to find love and lose it," her grandmother's voice echoed, the words laced with sorrow, with regret, as though they held a weight, a burden she had carried, a burden she had passed down to Dahlia, a curse that would haunt her through every life, through every love. "It will repeat itself, over and over. You will find him, you will lose him, and you will find him again."

Dahlia's hands shook, her breath coming in shallow gasps as the weight of her fate pressed down on her, filling her with a dread that left her feeling as though she were drowning, as though she were standing on the edge of an abyss, staring into a darkness that was hers alone, a darkness she could never escape.

She looked up, her gaze meeting her grandmother's, her voice trembling as she spoke the words that had haunted her for as long as she could remember, the words that had driven her from her home, that had led her to this moment. "Why, Granmé?" she whispered, her voice breaking, her heart aching with a grief that went beyond words, beyond reason. "Why am I bound to this? Why can't I be free?"

Her grandmother's gaze hardened, her expression filled with an ancient, unbreakable sorrow. "You are bound to me, to our blood, to the land that made us," she said, her voice fierce, resonant, a force that filled the space around them. "You were born of Haiti's earth, forged by our ancestors' hands. But when you turned your back, when you left us for another life, you broke that sacred bond. Our blood doesn't forget. Our spirits don't forgive. You are a part of this, Dahlia, as much as it is a part of you— and the bond that ties you here can never be cut."

The room faded, the shadows closing in, pressing down, filling the air with a weight that left Dahlia breathless, left her feeling as though she were being pulled apart, as though the very fabric of her soul were unraveling, leaving only fragments, only pieces of a life that had never truly been hers.

She opened her eyes, gasping as she found herself back in her own living room, the air thick, heavy, filled with the lingering scent of tobacco and coffee, a scent that brought with it a wave of memories, a wave of grief that left her feeling hollow, empty, as though a part of her had been stripped away, leaving only shadows, only echoes of the woman she had once been.

Dahlia sat on the cold, wooden floor of her living room, her breathing shallow as she tried to steady herself, her hands still trembling, her heart a frantic pulse in her chest. The lingering scent of tobacco and coffee drifted around her, the last traces of her grandmother's presence slipping away, leaving her alone in the silence, in the reality of what she now understood. Her hands dropped limply to her sides, and she let out a ragged breath, feeling the weight of the revelation settle over her, filling her with an emptiness she couldn't name.

"It is bound to you, and you are bound to it."

The words echoed in her mind, her grandmother's voice a haunting refrain that filled the quiet, pressing in on her, leaving her feeling raw, fragile, as though the very essence of her being had been stripped away, leaving only the bones of who she once was. The curse, the fate that had followed her through lifetimes, through loves she could barely remember, had bound her in ways she had never understood, ways she couldn't fight or deny.

A tear slipped down her cheek, warm against her skin, a reminder of the part of herself she had fought to hold onto, the part of herself that still clung to hope, that still believed, somehow, that there might be a way out. She wrapped her arms around herself, pulling her knees to her chest, feeling small, feeling human, as though the weight of her own body were too much to bear.

"Why...?" she whispered, her voice a broken plea, barely more than a breath, a question she knew would go unanswered. She could still feel Carlos's presence lingering, his face flickering in her mind, his touch a ghostly memory that left her aching, longing, even as she knew the truth—that he was part of the cycle, that he was bound to her by a force beyond their control, a force that would claim them both, over and over, without end.

Her hands clenched, her fingers digging into her arms as she fought against the helplessness that rose within her, a desperation that threatened to consume her, a longing that left her feeling as though she were standing on the edge of an abyss, staring into a darkness that offered no answers, no comfort, only the certainty of what lay ahead. And yet, even as she sat there, broken, vulnerable, she felt a flicker of something within her, a quiet, unyielding resolve, a determination that had carried her through lifetimes, that had brought her to this moment.

She wiped the tears from her cheeks, her gaze hardening as she took a steadying breath, feeling the weight of the curse, the weight of her grandmother's warning, settling over her, filling her with a grim understanding of the path before her. She didn't know how it would end, didn't know if she would find a way to break free, to escape the cycle that had claimed her, but she knew one thing—she wouldn't face it passively. She would meet it, head-on, with every ounce of strength she had left.

And as the last of the shadows faded, as the room grew quiet, Dahlia rose to her feet, her heart a steady, determined beat, her gaze fixed on the darkness beyond, ready to face whatever lay ahead, prepared, at last, for the final chapter of her story.

Chapter 13: Echoes of the Curse

Dahlia stood at the window, her gaze lost in the glow of the city lights, though her mind was far from the quiet hum of the streets below. The weight of her grandmother's voice, the stern warning wrapped in an ancient curse, had wound itself around her, sinking deeper with every hour. The same curse had bound her to Carlos, and now it threatened to tear them apart again.

She heard his footsteps before he even knocked. A tight knot formed in her chest, her pulse quickening as she waited, unsure of what to say, how to even begin explaining the tangled reality that lay between them. When the knock finally came, she hesitated for a beat before opening the door.

Carlos's face was shadowed and tense. The usual warmth in his eyes had been replaced by a troubled, almost frantic look, as if he were fighting an internal battle just to be there.

"Carlos," she said softly, her voice barely more than a whisper.

He stepped inside, the tension between them thick and heavy. He studied her for a moment, his gaze searching her face, as if trying to find answers to questions he hadn't dared to ask.

"Dahlia, I... I need to know," he began, his voice raw. "What's going on? I feel like I'm losing myself. Like... like I'm being pulled into something that I don't understand." He hesitated, his brow furrowing as he searched for the right words. "And it's not just you. Eve... she's different. She's not herself. It's like... like there's something dark hanging over us all."

The mention of Eve made Dahlia's heart clench. She knew, deep down, that the curse she'd tried to unleash on Eve had backfired in ways she couldn't control, leaving everyone around her caught in its grip.

"Carlos," she started, her voice trembling, her hands wringing together. "There are things... things I never wanted you to know. Things I didn't even want to believe myself."

"Then tell me, Dahlia!" His voice was louder now, filled with a frustration that bordered on anger. "I've tried to be patient, to give you space. But I feel like I'm caught in something I can't escape. Like every choice I make is pushing me closer to... to losing everything." His voice softened, the anger giving way to desperation. "Please, Dahlia. I just... I need to understand."

She looked down, unable to meet his gaze, the weight of her secrets pressing down on her, suffocating her. She took a deep breath, feeling the words catch in her throat. "It's... it's my family, Carlos. There's a curse. A curse that's bound to my blood, to my very soul."

He looked at her, disbelief flickering across his face. "A curse? Dahlia, what are you talking about?"

"It's true." She raised her gaze, meeting his eyes, pleading for him to believe her. "It's been passed down through generations. A curse that binds me to love, only to lose it. Every time I find someone... every time I think I've found happiness, it's taken from me." She swallowed hard, the pain of her words settling over her. "It's why I left Haiti, why I tried to leave everything behind. But it followed me, Carlos. It always follows me."

He took a step back, his face pale, his hands clenching and unclenching at his sides. "So... so this is it? We're just... just another chapter in some twisted story that you're trapped in?"

Her chest tightened, the sorrow she had tried to bury rising to the surface. "I never wanted this," she whispered, her voice breaking. "I wanted to be free, to find love on my own terms. But the curse... it's stronger than I am. Stronger than anything I've ever known."

Carlos shook his head, his expression a mixture of horror and disbelief. "And what about Eve?" he asked, his voice barely more than a whisper. "Is she... is she caught up in this too?"

Dahlia's gaze dropped to the floor, guilt washing over her. "I tried to stop it," she murmured, the words barely audible. "I tried to break free, to keep her out of it. But... the curse has a way of finding its own path."

He took a shaky breath, his hands running through his hair as he tried to process her words. "So what now?" he asked, his voice filled with a quiet desperation. "Are we just... supposed to give up? Accept that this... this curse is going to destroy everything?"

She looked at him, her own desperation mirrored in his gaze. "I don't know, Carlos," she admitted, her voice thick with grief. "I've spent my whole life running from this, trying to find a way out. But every time I think I'm free, it finds me again."

He closed his eyes, his shoulders sagging as the weight of her words settled over him. When he spoke, his voice was a broken whisper. "I thought... I thought we had a chance. That maybe... maybe we could be different."

Dahlia felt her own heart break at his words, the hope she had held onto slipping through her fingers. "So did I," she murmured, her voice barely audible. "But I don't know if love is enough to break the cycle."

They stood in silence, the truth hanging heavy between them, a truth that neither of them could escape, a truth that had bound them together, only to tear them apart.

Carlos took a deep breath, his gaze hardening as he looked at her. "Then maybe it's time to end this," he said, his voice steady, a quiet resolve settling over him.

She looked at him, her heart pounding as she took in his words, a glimmer of hope flickering in the depths of her despair. "What do you mean?"

He stepped closer, his hands reaching out to take hers, his gaze fierce, unwavering. "Maybe we can break the curse, Dahlia," he murmured, his voice filled with a determination she hadn't seen before. "Maybe... if we're strong enough, if we fight hard enough... we can find a way out."

She looked at him, a mixture of fear and hope swirling within her, the possibility of freedom within reach, and yet still so far away. "And what if we can't?" she asked, her voice trembling, her own fear creeping back in.

Carlos's grip tightened, his gaze unwavering. "Then at least we'll go down fighting," he replied, his voice firm. "Together."

She felt a tear slip down her cheek, a mixture of relief and sorrow filling her as she looked at him, the man who had become her salvation and her damnation, the man who was willing to risk everything to break free of the cycle that had bound them.

And in that moment, as they stood together, hands clasped, the weight of the curse pressing down on them, they both knew the truth. That no matter what lay ahead, no matter the cost, they would face it together.

Because love, even a love bound by a curse, was worth fighting for.

Chapter 14: The Cycle Reborn

Dahlia's hands trembled as she gathered the final ingredients, her gaze fixed on the leather-bound book laid open before her. The spell written across its yellowed pages felt like a living thing, pulsing with energy, filling the room with a sense of foreboding. Her heart pounded as she took a deep breath, forcing herself to focus, to still the fear that coiled in her stomach. This ritual was unlike any she'd attempted. It was ancient, dangerous, a calling to the spirits of her ancestors—and she knew, deep down, that it would either free her or bind her more tightly than ever before.

She moved to the center of the room, the symbols of her family's bloodline etched on the floor in a thick ring of salt, herbs, and ashes. Dahlia lit a candle and poured oils over her hands, feeling the warmth seep into her skin, steadying her as she began the incantation. Her voice was low, a whisper at first, filled with reverence as she called upon the spirits of her ancestors, those who had come before her, those who had carried this curse.

"Spirits of my blood, hear my plea. Granmé, I summon you," she intoned, her voice growing stronger, deeper, filling the silence, the air around her growing thick, charged. "By our bond, by my blood, come forth and grant me release, grant me freedom from this unending cycle."

The room darkened, shadows creeping along the walls, pooling around her as the air filled with the scent of tobacco, incense, and herbs. Her skin prickled as a chill swept over her, a sensation that sank deep, curling around her bones, filling her with a cold that went beyond physical, a cold that seemed to reach into her very soul.

As she continued chanting, her body began to feel heavy, her limbs numb, as though the weight of her ancestors' spirits had settled over her, pressing down, surrounding her. She closed her eyes, focusing on her voice, her breath, her will, letting it flow through her, binding her to the ritual, to the spell she had set in motion.

"Granmé…" she whispered, her voice breaking as she felt a presence take shape before her. She opened her eyes, her breath catching as she saw her grandmother's face, etched in shadows, her gaze sharp, filled with a sorrow and a strength that took Dahlia's breath away.

"You seek what cannot be undone," her grandmother's voice echoed, deep, resonant, vibrating through her bones. "You call upon us for freedom, but freedom is not without cost."

"I am willing," Dahlia said, her voice trembling but resolute, her hands clenched at her sides. "I have loved, and I have lost. I have lived with this curse long enough. I am ready to pay the price, whatever it is."

Her grandmother's gaze softened, her eyes dark, filled with a sorrow that left Dahlia feeling exposed, vulnerable, as though her very soul were laid bare. "You do not understand the weight of the curse you bear, the depth of the bond that binds you. It is more than love, more than loss. It is the blood of our line, a bond that stretches beyond time, beyond life."

Dahlia's breath hitched, her hands shaking as she felt the full weight of her grandmother's words settle over her, filling her with a dread that went beyond fear, beyond reason. She felt herself sinking, her mind slipping away, the room fading as she was pulled into the depths of the vision, the past unfolding around her.

She was standing in a forest, the trees towering above her, their branches heavy with moss, the air thick with the scent of earth and rain. She looked down, seeing her own hands, younger, different, holding a dagger etched with symbols she didn't recognize, symbols that pulsed with an energy that felt ancient, powerful. And there, standing before her, was Carlos. His face was different, the lines softer, his eyes a shade darker, but it was him— she knew it, felt it in her bones.

They locked eyes, and she felt a surge of emotion, a love that went beyond words, beyond time, a love that filled her with a longing that was both beautiful and devastating.

"Dahlia..." he whispered, his voice filled with a tenderness that made her heart ache. "We're... we're not meant to be. You know that."

She shook her head, tears streaming down her face as she raised the dagger, her hands trembling. "I can't lose you," she murmured, her voice thick with grief. "I can't..."

The vision shifted, the forest dissolving around her, replaced by the flickering candlelight of a grand ballroom. She was standing in a flowing gown, her hand resting in his as they moved in time with the music, their gazes locked, a promise unspoken between them. But even in that moment, she saw the sorrow in his eyes, a sorrow that mirrored her own, a sorrow that told her they were living on borrowed time, that this love, like all the others, was doomed to end.

Another shift, and she was standing on a battlefield, the sound of clashing swords filling the air, her heart racing as she searched for him, her eyes scanning the chaos, desperate to find him. And then she saw him, his face pale, his body broken, his life slipping away as he reached out for her, his hand falling just short, his gaze filled with a love that would never die, a love that would follow her, that would find her, over and over again.

The visions came faster now, each one a fragment of a life she had lived, a love she had lost, each one a reminder of the cycle that bound them, the cycle she was trying so desperately to break. She felt herself slipping, her mind unraveling as the weight of centuries pressed down on her, each life, each love, each loss, filling her with a grief that went beyond words, beyond time.

And then, in the midst of the swirling memories, she felt his presence beside her, his hand warm against hers, grounding her, pulling her back to the present. She looked up, her gaze meeting his, and she saw the understanding in his eyes, the pain, the longing, the realization that they were bound together, that their souls were entwined, no matter how many lives they lived, no matter how many times they found each other, only to lose each other.

"Dahlia," he murmured, his voice filled with a quiet desperation. "What... what is this?"

She took a deep breath, her hand tightening around his, her voice trembling as she spoke. "This... this is us, Carlos. This is what we've been living, over and over, lifetime after lifetime. We're... we're cursed, bound to find each other, only to lose each other."

He looked at her, his gaze filled with a mixture of disbelief and sorrow, his voice barely more than a whisper. "And... and there's no way to end it?"

She shook her head, her heart breaking as she looked at him, the man she had loved in a thousand different ways, in a thousand different lives, the man she was bound to, no matter how many times they found each other, no matter how many times they lost each other. "I don't know," she murmured, her voice filled with a quiet despair. "But I'm going to try. For us."

He nodded, his hand warm against hers, his gaze filled with a quiet determination. "Then I'm with you, Dahlia. No matter what it takes."

The shadows around them began to fade, the vision slipping away, leaving them standing in the dimly lit apartment, the weight of their shared history pressing down on them, filling the silence with a grief that went beyond words, beyond time.

And as they stood there, hands clasped, hearts intertwined, they both felt the truth settle over them, a truth they couldn't escape, a truth that bound them, no matter how many lives they lived, no matter how many times they tried to break free.

For they were bound, bound by love, bound by loss, bound by a cycle that would never end.

As the last remnants of the vision dissolved, Dahlia found herself kneeling on the floor, her breath ragged, her body drained of all warmth. She glanced down at her hands, faint smudges of ash and salt tracing her fingers, symbols of a ritual that had brought her to the edge of reality and beyond. Around her, the shadows seemed to pulse, filled with the whispered voices of her ancestors, fading but ever-present.

She turned slowly, her gaze locking onto Carlos. His face was pale, his eyes haunted, yet calm, as though he too had glimpsed the magnitude of their fate, the full weight of their history together. In his gaze, she saw love, unwavering and steady, but also resignation—a quiet understanding that echoed the truth they both now understood.

Carlos took a step forward, reaching for her hand, and as his fingers intertwined with hers, she felt a surge of warmth, a final embrace that would stay with her, even as the cycle slipped them away from each other. She leaned into him, their foreheads touching, their breaths mingling in the charged silence that settled around them. Words felt unnecessary; everything she needed to say, he already knew, as deeply and irrevocably as she did.

"Carlos," she whispered, her voice trembling. "This is goodbye, isn't it?"

He nodded, his voice catching. "Maybe... but maybe we'll find each other again." His tone held a fragile hope, though they both knew the truth—a truth as inevitable as it was heartbreaking.

They held each other for a long moment, the world outside fading, leaving only the two of them suspended in the weight of this final encounter, bound by love and loss in equal measure.

Finally, as though some unseen force tugged at the fabric of reality, the shadows began to shift, stretching and pulling them apart. The candles flickered, their flames dwindling to faint embers, casting long, fading shadows across the room.

Carlos's image blurred, fading before her eyes, his hand slipping from hers as he took a step back, his face a blend of sorrow and acceptance.

"Dahlia..." he murmured, his voice soft, a final echo that lingered in the quiet. "I'll see you again."

And then, in a single heartbeat, he was gone, leaving her standing alone, the silence closing in around her, the familiar weight of the curse settling once more over her shoulders.

A tear slipped down her cheek, her heart aching with a grief that spanned centuries, yet as she took a trembling breath, she felt a strange calm, a quiet acceptance of the path that lay before her. She had tried, fought against her fate with all she had, and though the cycle remained unbroken, she knew now that the love she shared with Carlos would live on, hidden in the shadows of time, waiting to emerge once more.

With one last glance around the dim room, she whispered a quiet goodbye, her voice filled with the strength of all the lives she had lived, all the love she had carried, and then, as the last of the candlelight faded, she closed her eyes, letting the cycle take her, her spirit slipping into the silence, ready to begin again.

Chapter 1: Full Circle

The morning sunlight filtered through the café's large windows, casting a soft golden glow across the tables, filling the space with a warm, welcoming light. Dahlia adjusted her apron, smoothing it over her waist as she moved with familiar purpose behind the counter, her gaze shifting to the entrance out of habit. The café buzzed with the usual hum of morning energy: the rhythmic clatter of cups and silverware, quiet conversations rising and falling, the faint whir of the espresso machine. Today felt like any other day, yet something subtle, something almost unnameable, hung in the air.

A strange sensation prickled at the edge of her awareness, a vague feeling that today was different, that something awaited her just beyond her grasp. She glanced down at the day's orders, catching herself mid-thought, shaking off the feeling as just a remnant of a restless night. Yet as she continued her tasks, the sensation persisted, leaving her with the sense that something important was about to happen.

She adjusted the coffee grinder, watching the dark beans spill down into the machine. The aroma rose around her, rich and familiar, grounding her as she lost herself in the simple, soothing routine of the morning. She poured a fresh batch of coffee, the warm liquid filling the cup as her mind drifted, her fingers moving in practiced motions as she prepared the orders, though her thoughts were elsewhere, tugged by a vague anticipation she couldn't place.

The bell above the door chimed, and instinctively, Dahlia looked up, her heart skipping a beat as a man stepped into the café. He paused just inside the doorway, his gaze sweeping over the room, and as his eyes met hers, a peculiar jolt shot through her, a flicker of recognition that left her breathless. He seemed to hesitate for a moment, as though caught by the same strange pull, his gaze lingering on her, intense and thoughtful.

Something about him tugged at her, an inexplicable sense of familiarity that made her chest tighten. She didn't know his name, didn't recognize his face, and yet... there was a feeling, an almost electric charge in the air between them, as if they had shared something beyond this moment, something she couldn't remember but felt in her bones.

He approached the counter, his footsteps steady, confident, yet his expression was softened by a warmth that set her pulse racing. She reached for her pen and pad, her fingers brushing against the smooth surface of the counter, grounding herself as she tried to calm the flutter of her heartbeat.

"Good morning," he said, his voice low and warm, the sound carrying a note of easy familiarity that unsettled her in ways she couldn't explain. "Could I get a coffee, please?"

Her own voice felt steady as she responded, though a hint of nervousness crept in. "Of course," she said, her fingers tightening slightly around the pen. "How do you take it?"

"Black," he replied, a small smile curving his lips as he met her gaze, a hint of amusement sparking in his eyes. "Nothing added."

She nodded, her hands moving to the coffee machine, but she was acutely aware of his presence, the way his gaze lingered on her, as if he were searching for something he couldn't quite place. As she poured his coffee, the strange sensation grew, an intensity that wrapped around her like a cocoon, filling her with a strange, aching familiarity. Her hands shook slightly as she placed the cup on the counter, her fingers brushing against his as he took it from her, a brief contact that sent a shiver up her spine.

"Thank you," he murmured, his voice soft, his gaze holding hers a beat too long, his expression shifting to something thoughtful, almost wistful.

"You're welcome," she replied, her own voice quiet, a tremor of something unnameable underlying the words. She watched him as he moved to a nearby table, settling himself in the corner, his attention seemingly absorbed in his coffee, though she felt his gaze flicker back to her now and then, each glance sparking a rush of warmth in her chest.

As the minutes ticked by, she tried to immerse herself in her work, but her thoughts kept drifting back to him, the feeling lingering like an aftertaste she couldn't shake. She found herself stealing glances in his direction, each look confirming the feeling that this man, this stranger, was somehow important, though she couldn't say why or how. Her heart beat a little faster each time their eyes met, a silent exchange passing between them, as though they shared a secret they were both trying to remember.

The morning rush continued, customers filtering in and out, but her attention remained divided, drawn inexplicably toward him.

She felt the weight of his presence, an unspoken connection that left her feeling as though the rest of the world had faded, leaving only the two of them suspended in this quiet, charged moment.